Clocktower Books
San Diego

Special Pocket Edition of

Lethal Journey

❧ Historical Thriller ❧
1892 Gaslamp True Crime & Ghost Legend

By

John T. Cullen

Closely based on a true story, as revealed in the
author's detailed analysis in <u>Dead Move: Kate
Morgan and the Haunting Mystery of Coronado</u>

Available online and in bookstores—print and digital Editions

www.sandiegoauthor.com/

Clocktower Books, Publisher
P.O. Box 600973
Grantville Station
San Diego, California 92160-0973
www.clocktowerbooks.com

editorial@clocktowerbooks.com

Images in this book are from the 1800s, in the public domain, and easily found online. Exception: the background and rose on the cover are from the author's photos. The young woman's image is from an 1800s St. Valentine's Day card—artist unknown; public domain.

JOHN T. CULLEN

LETHAL JOURNEY

A NOVEL BASED ON A TRUE STORY

Dedication

To
Carolyn and Andrew
As always
And to
Elizabeth 'Lizzie' Wyllie
(c1868-1892)
The quintessentially classic and tragic
Victorian Fallen Angel

Special Thanks to our intrepid, detail-oriented editor, Sarah Dawson, for a great job on every line of this manuscript. Contact Mrs. Dawson at **WordPlay Editing** by email at **sdawson@wordplayediting.com**. The editorial website is

www.wordplayediting.com.

Special thanks to 1SG Richard Agler, USMC-Ret. for invaluable information regarding hand guns, ballistics, and related issues about the gun found near the violently and mysteriously deceased Elizabeth 'Lizzie' Wyllie's hand.

Elizabeth 'Lizzie' Wyllie was the Beautiful Stranger, who has ever since gained fame as the ghost of the Hotel del Coronado under various false or wrongly attributed names including 'Kate Morgan' and 'Lottie A. Bernard.' When her unexplained death became a national sensation in 1892, the press called her 'The Beautiful Stranger,' a name still used in official publications of the Hotel del Coronado in the twenty-first century. Based on the most famous, contradictory feminine ideal and nadir of her age, she is the incarnation of Thomas Hardy's Tess of the D'Urbervilles, and other Victorian Fallen Angels.

Table of Contents

1. Kate & Tom Morgan, 1888

Two men, reeking of leather and tobacco, stood in the shade of a wooden awning at the small train station in Las Cruces, New Mexico. On this hot summer day in 1888, with tiny gusts of oven-like wind pushing through the ivy trellises around the wooden train platform, the two men looked as if they were not enjoying themselves much. On the other hand, they looked too busy to care much about their discomfort as they pored over a map together, while one of them held a packet of tear sheets with images and print on them. Wind rattled the paper every few seconds. The land all around was flat and far and baked like painted mud. Both men were tall, about the same height, and lean. Thinning hair stirred in white strands on a browned and blistered head when each removed his head gear to scratch. One man had a salt-and-pepper beard; the other, gray stubble over a mass of wrinkles around his mouth. Beard had dark brown eyes. The other was gray-eyed.

Each man, under his rumpled black suit, wore a shiny brass badge discreetly on his leather belt under a flap of his jacket. Each man's badge bore a plain, engraved personal number in the center. Fancy scrollwork, around the number, read *Union Pacific* and *Railroad Police*. On the other side of the leather belt, under the opposite jacket flap, each man wore a shiny, nickel-plated 1888 Remington New Model Pocket Army Revolver with .44 caliber Winchester rounds in the cylinder, and a short 5.5 inch barrel. Each man wore a broad-brimmed hat covered with dust from a long ride on horseback, but they had traded their riding boots for stiff-soled city shoes. The men were on the hunt, just the same, only their hunting territory was coming toward them. They heard a distant train whistle, and were eager to get on board and search for quarry. Each good arrest meant a bonus. They worked hard for their money.

"I'll send the boots out for cleaning," hollered an elderly black man in shirtsleeves and great big boots, who puffed a corncob pipe and moved at a leisurely pace as he led the two tired horses toward a barn to be wiped down and watered. Man and horses both looked husky and sun-beaten.

The bearded detective gave a little wave of thanks, as if his every motion must be spare and economical. The hand that waved wore a scuffed, fine chocolate-colored leather glove whose index finger had been removed—leaving the business end of his finger exposed, when it needed to be, on the hair-trigger of his six-shooter. Both men were Civil War veterans in their late forties. Each had killed men and faced death enough times to get that dark, lean, haunted look around the eyes that was like a permanent shadow, a veil of nightmares.

The two men rifled through their assortment of Wanted posters, trying to memorize faces and read details. They had just ridden in from Santa Fe, where they had delivered two bank robbers and collected a hefty fee aside from their regular salary. Now they were ready for a new hunt.

"These two," said Gray-Eyes as he pulled a fresh tear sheet from Beard's gloved hand. "They're new."

"Ah-yuh," said Beard. "That's a new one. Should be easy to spot if they're working as a pair."

They looked at lithographic reproductions of the profiles of a young man and woman. Under the pictures were names in bold, black print: Thomas E. Morgan and Kate Morgan, born Farmer. Under that was printed, in smaller letters, a list of charges, including that they were cardsharps. Missing was the next line that appeared in some other sheets: *Caution! Armed!*—so evidently these were light-weights. Then came the small print, citing any known details about the two. As Beard and Gray-Eyes read, the distant train whistle drew near. Already, they could hear the chuffing of the engine as the coal-burner came racing through a distant mountain range. From experience, they could assemble a small drama in their imaginations.

કર્ ભ્

*T*homas Edward Morgan and his wife, Kate Morgan, were grifters who worked the Transcontinental Railroad trains. Tom was in his early 30s, while Kate was nearly ten years his junior. They hailed from the wheat belt in southwest Iowa, children of well-to-do farming and miller families. Somehow, they hadn't set well—the land apparently had no lure for them, and they preferred to travel. Once the railroad bug got you, there was no turning back.

Typically, Kate would find a mark—some young man with a few whiskeys in him already, a gullible mind, and a fat wallet. She'd entice him into a deserted forward car, where the spider waited in his web: Tom Morgan, grinning easily under his short black hair, riffling a deck of cards. Tom would give the impression of sipping at a shot of Red Canary Straight Rye Whiskey from a colorful bottle that stood nearly full and invitingly at his elbow. "I want you to meet my brother," Kate would tell their intended victim as she ushered him into the compartment. "I hope he will like you, because he is a good judge of men, and you seem like a fine gentleman." She had the poor fool thinking, in his muddled mind, that he would somehow have his way with her in the next few days as the train clattered monotonously through the endless Continental United States. As the mark slid into his seat opposite Tom Morgan, the latter would reach into his coat for a silver etui and offer him a fresh cigar. Kate would sit in a corner and continue flirting with the man while Tom invited him to a friendly little game of poker. "You get to know a man when you play cards with him," Tom would say. "Looks like my sister here has taken a shine to you." Then he'd riffle the deck some more, and the game was on.

The two railroad policemen folded away their posters and stepped out to the edge of the platform, each carrying a dark and ornately decorated cloth valise. Gray-Eyes' was dark green with maroon swirls, while Beard's was dark blue with gold lines in a Romanesque motif. The train was growing louder now, and its smoke filled the sky in quick, energetic bursts. The smoke stack on the front of the dark-green locomotive was a wide cinder-catcher type, designed to prevent hot ashes from flying back and setting the cars on fire. Meanwhile, the grating in front was designed to toss aside the carcass of any stray cow unlucky enough to be wandering on the tracks. The train emitted a series of piercing steam-whistle notes, rising and falling, while the wheels chattered happily until the last mile or so, when they started to slow and the train started sounding tired. The old black man came from the stable, in that same lethargic middle-of-nowhere walk, and pulled the hose pipe around on a high wooden water tower. A trio of young Indian lads, wearing good cotton shirts and Levi Strauss work pants with suspenders, and a variety of top hats with feathers and beaded designs, pulled a wagon of coal and wood along a narrow-gauge side track nearby.

A Mexican vendor appeared on the platform with cigars, sandwiches, and fruits, while his wife and children struggled alongside with a clay coffee urn and tin cups. The train's great steel wheels screeched on the steel rails as the train chuffed slowly to a halt on air brakes. The engineers leaned from their cab, and a conductor in a dark blue uniform waved to them. The two detectives looked like traveling salesmen as they quietly boarded amid two dozen or so passengers milling about, some getting on, others getting off. A woman cried and waved her hankie as she spoke in Spanish to two brown-skinned boys with big eyes in school uniforms. A young wife waved to her Army officer husband who leaned from a window throwing kisses. Arms reached out to the Mexican, placing coins in his hand and accepting coffee, food, tobacco, even tiny paper flags with local motifs for souvenirs.

Coaled and watered within a half hour, the train emitted a shrill whistling sound. The engine pumped, and chuffed, and began its pile-driver rhythm to propel tons of steel and wood back to speed. The two detectives deposited their satchels in the railroad caboose at rear, and started a leisurely walk down the train. They kept their coats buttoned to conceal the purpose of their journey. There was no rush now. The several hundred passengers were safely imprisoned in a world of hurtling upholstery and dusty glass windows. Mesilla Valley cotton acreage passed by outside, looking like fields of snow. The sky was a cloudless darkish blue, raked by the summer sun and hot desert winds. Low mountains looked as if they had white cake-patterns baked into them. The rocking motion of the train was steady and hypnotic. The men sidled among passengers who crowded the aisle outside First Class and Second Class compartments. They moved through the bar coach and into the restaurant.

Suddenly, Beard gripped Gray-Eyes' sleeve. They froze in place, looking over the heads of a school of dark-haired children, toward a row of dining seats. Two black men in white coats served coffee and cakes to a white family seated around a long table. Beyond them, seated together in a corner, were the Morgan couple. They were unmistakable from their pictures—he with the slightly bulbous, pale head and short dark hair; she with the piercing black eyes and rather plain features. She did not have a pretty face, but she had the scintillating gaze and golden tongue of a first-class seductress. Their clothing was dark, thin for the summer, and dusty. Under a plaid blouse and ankle-length tan cotton skirt, her figure was full and robust, promising much to a gullible and slightly inebriated man looking for a place to shed his dollars. She wore a little gold locket around her neck, which she often fingered and then stuck down into her blouse for its protection. Her husband, the sibling in their brother-sister act, had the strong, wiry lean build of a Midwest farmer. He had probably been a towheaded youngster, Beard thought as he and Gray-Eyes withdrew into the shadows of the new leather accordion connectors between cars. Morgan glanced toward them for a second, then looked away.

"We'll split up," Beard said quietly. Something in that man's eyes made him nervous. The woman's were just as unsettling. Gray-Eyes nodded. They would be less conspicuous apart. The couple weren't supposed to be dangerous, and the bounty on them would be relatively small. If the detectives could apprehend them, especially in the act, with a witness and complainant, they could turn them in at the sheriff's office in some town up the road and then continue looking for bigger game.

"We're in luck," Beard said in the same low voice. "You go back to the rear and get some rest. We'll spell each other." Gray-Eyes nodded and walked leisurely off without looking around. Beard picked up a discarded, folded newspaper, and shadowed the couple as they made their way forward to an empty first-class carriage. This car did not have wood or glass dividers, but the compartments had fine, plush blue-gray seats with high backs that served like dividers. Half the coach was, in fact, a sleeper with darkened, empty bunk slots. Beard sat in a corner booth and opened his paper on the table. He watched from a distance, in window reflections, as a bottle appeared on a small window table and Tom Morgan set up his gambling ruse. Kate, meanwhile, wandered in search of just the right man with a few itches to scratch. As she passed by, Beard looked up from his newspaper and exchanged looks with her. He made himself seem distant, as if his thoughts were elsewhere. She languidly raked him with a carnal gaze. A chill ran up and down his spine. He felt as if he were being licked by a snake. He shuddered and looked away.

She passed him by because he had not radiated toward her the spark of hunger and gullibility for which she was looking. After a few minutes, he rose. Folding his newspaper under one arm, and pruning a cigar with his pocket knife, he wandered after her. The bar car was crowded with mostly men, a few women joining their husbands at window seats. Women were not allowed at the bar.

Beard watched as Kate approached a fortyish, plump man with short, graying hair parted on one side, and a checkered vest. The man was reading a Denver newspaper and tossing back shots of whiskey while fingering a coffee cup to one side and keeping a cigar going in the smoky car air. The man was florid and had little watery blue eyes as he began to notice Kate. She pretended to be looking for some acquaintance. They caught each other's eyes, and spoke to one another. She probably said she was looking for her 'brother.' After a few more words, he eagerly rose and offered her a seat opposite him at the small table. He was very solicitous, putting his cigar out and using his napkin to dust the glass counter top. He bowed slightly and said something, probably offering her a drink or coffee, and she protested, but he protested more, and she relented as he signaled for a waiter. Soon, one of the black stewards in starchy white linen vest brought a tea service for her, and another stiff drink for him.

Beard sauntered back to get Gray-Eyes. He picked up his step as soon as he was out of sight, and was fairly trotting by the time he hurried through the crowded third class coaches with their teeming families of all races. Entering the caboose, which smelled of sawdust and machine oil—no passenger comforts—he went down the row of canvas bunks hanging on steel poles. He found a bunk with Gray-Eyes' jacket curled as a pillow and still warm —but no Gray-Eyes. A Chinese porter happened by, wearing a *chignon* and round black hat, and an ankle-length blue apron. Beard pointed to the bunk. The porter pointed to the locked toilet door in a corner and grinned. Beard pounded on the door. "They're starting."

The other shouted back distantly: "I'm going to be busy here for the next few minutes. That Mexican food is going through me like a train."

"Hurry up," Beard said, laughing. "I can hear your train whistle."

"Oh shut up and go do your job."

"Join me when you're able." Beard took his time walking forward to the eerily deserted Tom Morgan coach. He passed through the bar and restaurant coaches. He'd wait for Gray-Eyes to join him. The Morgans would need a while to work their cardsharp game. The trick would be in the timing—they needed the victim as a willing witness.

Beard watched Kate sipping her tea and making pleasant conversation with her mark. Beard studied her, trying to figure out how she worked her magic. It was rather chilling, he found. She was a bit homely, but she could turn up this warm, radiant smile that made her eyes and lips sparkle. She also moved her foot close, so that the man's ankle brushed against hers. The man, for his part, was rapt. He sat forward, with his arms folded under his flabby chest in that suit, and seemed to be inhaling the very essence of her smiles and sweet words. Beard saw the ankle-action and thought to himself: *I wonder if he's wondering if she's doing it on purpose, or if she doesn't know, and he's wondering just how far she'll let him go with her, and how much it's going to cost him*.

Then, after about twenty minutes of that, they rose and she followed him out of the bar car. Then, in the corridor, she stepped ahead to guide him. He was a heavy man, and leaned a bit with one hand against the wall as he navigated in his cups. At one point, he reached out and tried to touch her rear end in its hoop skirt, but stumbled and almost fell on his face. She turned with a look of phony concern and took his arm. With this new, seemingly innocuous body contact, she lured him to the compartment where Tom sat waiting. Beard noticed a reddish bruise on one cheek, as if Morgan had given his wife a black eye recently. Morgan looked the type, Beard thought, a flinty-eyed, mean-spirited confidence artist.

Beard watched from a distance as the heavy-set man sat down opposite Tom, while Kate sat nearby and smiled at the man with that same magical, balmy look that had him eating from her hands. Tom deliberately took his time. He poured the man a shot and pushed it toward him. The victim began to lose his shyness and become part of what must have seemed like a family to him. Brother and sister, they were utterly warm, simple, charming, seductive, and friendly. Tom spread out a hand of cards and tapped the deck with his forefinger. It didn't matter what the game was. Maybe the victim didn't even know how to play cards. The ruse was that the brother must approve of the man before he would allow his sister to become more friendly with him. Beard supposed that the victim by now thought that these two odd ducks were maybe a pair of simpletons (never mind the cigars, booze, and cards) and that a license from Tom would give him entry to the paradise that Kate subliminally promised. Beard could feel it all the way across the coach, from his spy place near the connector—a radiant emanation that snared its victim in a net of coquettish nods, and glances, and smiles, and turning aside of the head in pretended shyness.

Gray-Eyes came up behind Beard and startled him. Beard said, "Just in time. The wolves are closing in on their lamb."

"Looks like the wolves have him cornered."

"They're feeding him whiskey, and I wouldn't be surprised if she's dropped some magic powder in his glass to hurry it up."

Gray-Eyes clutched his stomach. "Oh no."

"Make it quick," Beard said.

Gray-Eyes hurried away to find a toilet.

Within a few minutes, the victim began to seem torpid. First, he stopped moving and just sat like a big frozen slab of lard. His eyes grew confused and the cards tumbled from his fat white fingers. Beard knew then—Tom Morgan had slipped him a dose of something. The heavy man snapped his head upright two or three times, but finally sank into a deep slumber. Kate hurried to his side and helped him lie down on the seat. Both Morgans were all over him in an instant, going through his pockets. As Tom Morgan triumphantly held up the man's black leather wallet, Beard pulled his coat back and stepped into the middle of the cabin, displaying his badge on the left and his gun on the right. "Hold it right there, both of you. You're under arrest."

"What for?" said Kate with a big smile. "Our friend here has had too much to drink."

"With a little help from you two," Beard said.

"What is the matter with you?" Tom asked. "Are you crazy?"

"I was just about to ask you that," Beard said. He reached into his coat pocket and pulled out a chain with a shiny steel handcuff on each end. The very next instant, he knew he had terribly miscalculated.

Tom Morgan had two Deringers, one in each hand, now aimed at

Beard's head and torso. Tom stood at a slight crouch, holding the pistols at slightly different angles with the practiced stance of one who was no newcomer at this. "Mister, I don't know who you are, but you're looking at the Angel of Death."

"Take it easy," said Beard as he raised his gloved hands halfway and opened them in hapless surrender.

"Now we just have minutes here, don't we? Before a porter comes through, or your friend returns. I thought you two looked suspicious. Kate, put the manacles on him."

"You are digging yourself a hole," Beard said.

"Stow the big talk. I'll kill you right here, right now, if I have to. Got nothing to lose if it comes to that."

As he spoke, Beard could feel the woman move around him. He heard the chain rattle, and felt the sharp bite of a manacle on his right wrist. "Hands behind you," she snapped. He offered his other wrist to cuff.

"Okay, Mister," said Tom Morgan. "You can avoid meeting Jesus today if you don't waste any more of my time and just do what I say."'

"Fair enough," Beard said, knowing he was licked.

"Kate," Tom said. She pushed Beard toward Tom. Morgan pocketed one gun and kept the other trained on Beard's head. The man and woman led Beard toward the door, and Beard understood what was coming next. Tom said: "You play along, you just got yourself a long, thirsty walk to the nearest town. You screw with me, and I'll throw you out there with a bullet in your head. Make up your mind."

The door swung open at Kate's push. Wind howled by, and made their hair and clothes rattle. Beard's hat flew away. Dusty grit swirled in circles that made all three persons blink. They spat harsh dust from between their teeth. As Kate and Tom watched, Beard walked straight-up, as if he were stepping onto a train platform, out into the air, and instantly disappeared in a roar of wind. A glance behind told the two that their victim had landed, rolling, somewhere on the rocks and grit. "He'll be okay," Tom said as he kicked the hat after the man and pulled the door shut. "A little banged up and worse for wear, but he'll live. I shamed him. He won't say what happened to him here. "

"He'll be looking for us, though," she said. "There is another one, too."

"Yeah, I saw them both. You got the wallet?"

They looked at the sleeper. She said: "We got his watch, his money, his gold tie clip, his cuffs, his collar pin. We've cleaned him out."

"Good. Not a minute to waste. Act natural." Leaving the sleeper where he lay, they walked slowly back to the dining coaches. Tom kept his hands in his pockets, a Deringer in each fist. Kate clung to him, and he shook her off with an elbow to the ribs. "Woman, don't dog me now."

She held her side and grimaced in pain. "One day, I'm going to throw you off a train, you son of a bitch."

"You try me, woman, and you'll join that tin horn copper."

For a minute or two of menacing silence, they walked down the corridor of an empty car that was probably expected to fill up in some city ahead. On their left were windows overlooking desert and irrigated farm land. Several of the dusty windows were slightly open. In-rushing wind freshened the hallway's stale air, but brought with it dust and pollen, and a boiled-coal smell from the locomotive. On their right were closed and darkened cabins. Far ahead were the noise and laughter of the bar car.

As Tom and Kate approached a door marked *W.C.* on the right, the toilet door opened, with the hand of Gray-Eyes on the door handle. The man had finished his business, pulled up his pants, and was about to step out. One could hear the rattling of tracks under the open-bottomed box that dumped its contents on the ties as the train flew onward.

Tom saw the man's badge and gun and brought one of his Deringers up.

The lawman, with years of experience, took this all in during an instant. Lurching back, he reached for his gun. A collection of Wanted posters fluttered from under his elbow.

Tom shot him in the chest, and the policeman keeled over backwards onto the toilet seat. Tom glanced left and right, and saw that nobody had witnessed this. He put the Derringer in his pocket. He took the key from inside the door. The man sprawled, looking away with dull eyes, dying in a pool of blood, with his long legs crumpled and his arms extended to the sides as on a cross. Grabbing the Wanted posters, Tom pulled the door shut. He locked it from outside so that the white enamel sign said *Occupied*. He threw the key and the posters out the window.

Kate pointed ahead. "We're pulling into a town."

"Good. Let's lose ourselves. We've got the guy's money, and we'll figure out something—quickly hop a train going somewhere else." He put her arm under his elbow and grinned. "You still want to throw me off a train?"

She sighed, wrapped her arm around his, and gave him a rueful smile. Together, they waited by the nearest door for the train to stop so they could vanish into the enormous, empty continent that was their playground.

Tom and Kate Morgan stayed in Chicago for a time. They lived in a cheap apartment near the bay, in a third floor rear walkup with a rear landing and outside stairs. The place was a tenement, teeming night and day with screaming children, roaring drunks, and crying women. It was a veritable Babylon, with every tongue on earth being spoken.

The trains were too hot now to pull any schemes. Kate avidly followed the newspaper stories, reading them to Tom as they sat over coffee and toast for breakfast each morning.

The man Tom had forced to step off the train had landed and crushed his skull on a boulder, dying instantly. She felt a little pang in her gut as she read about this.

Elsewhere, she read about the man Tom had shot. After hours of silence, the toilet where the other railroad detective had died began to ooze a thick, dark liquid from under the door. Porters at first stepped over it and avoided it and told each other to get a mop and a bucket but nobody did, until they realized it did not stink like liquid feces but instead was cold, congealing blood. Tom and Kate were several states away before white-jacketed porters and the Chinaman broke down the door. The case was widely reported with the usual trumpeting of end-times and lax morality, but nobody really knew what had happened. The railroad issued a terse statement that the policemen had probably died in line of duty, since Wanted posters were strewn about the train tracks, but it wasn't clear who had murdered them. Nobody came forth to offer a clue.

Tom ate a ham sandwich while Kate sipped tea and read to him. Tom said: "Dammit, we have to lay low. And I need money."

"So?" Kate said. "I don't think anybody is on to us. Although it was rather stupid of you to throw the posters after the guy." As she often did, she nervously fingered the gold locket around her neck, and stuck it down her blouse for protection.

"Stupid?" Tom raged. "What choice did I have? What the hell is the matter with you? Do I see you carrying a gun? No, you depend on me to save and protect us both."

"Dear, you should have stopped to take our poster with us. Then they'd suspect all the others."

"Or, I take that one out, and they know it's us. Why don't you stick to your tea, and I'll stick to doing the thinking around here."

"Oh really, honey? And that's why we're sitting here in this dump, with breakfast but no lunch or dinner? Good job, honey."

He made a fist, as if he were going to hit her, and his eyes blazed, but bent angrily over his sandwich. "Go to hell."

She changed the subject, the way she always did when there was no reasoning with him. "So we stay off trains for a while. How long? A year? Two years?"

"I have an idea," he said. "Time for you to take another one of those temporary domestic jobs you're so good at."

"I don't have much choice, do I? I have an idea. You stay here and do all that thinking, and I'll go out to work and support us."

He reddened. "I'll support us, Kate. I'll go out and put my poker skills to use. You'll see. We'll do okay." His look appealed to her, reminding that they had been soul mates growing up in Iowa and ever since.

She sighed and put her paper down. "Oh, all right. Come here." She opened her arms with that raw sexuality she could radiate so intensely. He rushed around the table to kiss her. As they hugged, spoons and a salt shaker fell of the table. She ran her hands down his back to his buttocks. "Gimme," she said in a barely audible groan.

He uttered a groan of passion and lifted her to take her to bed. She pulled up her dress as he carried her, and with closed eyes and face turning side to side, gave him a stray thump on the chest. "Come on. "

He threw her down on the bed. She pulled up her knees and was ready for him, with her legs open. She taunted: "Are you man enough?"

He tore her underwear off along pale, smooth woman-legs. Her words rang around his ears, incomprehensible in the beating of his blood—she taunted, she begged, she cajoled.

Tossing her bloomers aside, he stared down into her as he furiously undid his belt and dropped his pants before crawling across the bed toward her. Her savage woman words rained down on him as he ran across the mattress on his knees to throw himself on her and silence her with the rage of his passion. She knew what was coming. She welcomed it. It was part of their rising to the fire, the way the sun rises from shadowy mountains in the morning and sets the sky aflame.

"Yeah!" she snarled, reaching for him with clawed fingers. Her eyes were dark orbs of desire and fury, her face a pale blur, her mouth a dark tear between wet rouge lips. He slapped her across the face, grazing a cheekbone. Stunned, she turned her face aside with the blow, but ready to take the rest of what he would give her. He tried to slap her firmly left, right, left, but she blocked his arm and pinned his wrists in her powerful hands. She spat at his face. His expression became something between rage and hunger. His eyes got huge. The corners of his mouth turned down, and his discolored teeth showed.

It was the only way she could enjoy letting a man take her. He had to defeat her, like an army climbing over ramparts in a hail of arrows. She wanted to be defeated and taken and spread open and ravaged with sex and love and passion. Her eyes fluttered as she recovered from the first blow. He squirmed around on her, grunting like a wild animal and pawing her wetness. Bracing herself, palms down, she made a bridge of her strong, firm, and ample body. She slammed her heels down repeatedly to bounce on the bed so that her bush struck his grasping palm, and wet slaps resounded through the room.

She sat astride him, still in her dress. She rode him like that for some intense minutes. He lay with his eyes closed, enjoying bliss. She felt like slapping him hard across the face in retaliation, but she knew he would go berserk and maybe forget about making love and beat her instead. In one impatient sweep, she pulled off her dress. It slid easily over her smooth, firm skin. She let it flutter away, and with it her slip. Her brassiere followed. "Grab them," she said tensely. He reached up to grasp the nurturing breasts she offered him, just for him, with thrusting nipples, and nut-dark areolas each studded with a circle of nubbins.

Her pale back was long and curving, shadowed along the *fossa* of her spine, her waist was full and firm, her buttocks were wide and creamy, her hair tumbled about as she turned her head from side to side in the rhythm of their unity. Tom pulled her gently down to nurse on her, and she grew patient as she looked at him and waited. They had been soul mates since adolescence. They had been making passionate love since long before their youthful marriage amid the grinding barrenness and intolerable boredom and then tragedy of their lives in Iowa. Nowadays, their sex was still always passionate, but the gaps between were growing ever more painful and alienating for her as Tom drank and grew moodier and more violent. He hurt her. He had murdered men, and was growing ever more dangerous, even for a woman like Kate, for whom his dangerous edge made a heady liquor. In the abandon of the love bed, that dark edge upped the ante, like when he pushed more money into one of his smoky poker games. But increasingly, except in little island moments of time like this, that intoxication grew harsh and repellent. Somewhere, deep in her soul, she knew a break was coming. Not now, not with him grasping her, mouth full, mewling under her in need as she suckled him and gently rode up and down on his hungry shaft. Not yet, but soon. She had no idea how or when, but the end seemed near. After that, she had no idea—she could not think beyond the moment. He cried out, forgetting her breasts. He held her by her sides and started thrusting in piston-quick motions. They wailed cacophonously as his savagely thrusting, bony hips slammed up at her in a frenzy, rocked her up and down. She cried out dizzily as they came together in an exhausting blur. Then they lay together, entwined, immobile, hung over from their passion and near unconsciousness as if glutted from a feast in the darkish room. As he snored on his back, she lay with her hands and chin on his chest, regarding the enigma she loved. The arch inside her thighs was gloriously sore, still trembling with the echoes of their unity. Her cheekbone, as it often did, throbbed as it swelled. She sighed deeply, and enjoyed the moment as if it were the last.

❧ ❦

K ate found temporary employment with a well-to-do family
who simply adored her because she was efficient, quiet,
and so very pleasant. She had done this before, when she and
Tom were short of money and his gambling was driving up
debts. It was a sweet system, really, and she saw great potential
to milk it. Once you got in—meaning, one family used you for a
week or two as a temporary domestic, usually because a prized
regular girl was sick or visiting her dying mother out of town,
once you had that foot in the door, there was a grapevine
among other wealthy ladies in town. If you were good—and
Kate, when she put her mind to it, was among the best, because
she knew it would only be for a week or two, and there was
money to be made—if you were good, you had no end of work.
You bounced from one home to the next, always changing
scenery, never bored. Kate started looking for opportunities, and
she discovered a new sideline for which she had a remarkable
talent. It was called blackmail, and it was a lot more lucrative
and less risky than robbing strangers on trains.

Tom was in a funk. When he got like this, she usually had him cool
off a while, just hang around and maybe stew over some long, slow
beers in the city's many taverns while she made a little honest
money as a nanny or a domestic and took whatever she could quietly
steal out the back door. A silver tea service might not be missed for
months until the next scheduled session when all the maids in a
wealthy house gathered in that room to open the cupboards and
have a polishing party—only to discover, with a shriek, that someone
had made off with the ornate centerpieces. Then they might rack
their brains over who had worked there the past few months, and
when this might have happened, and eventually would give up,
thinking maybe the pieces had never existed in the first place and it
was all in their imagination. A thorough scouring of all the pawn
shops and dealers for a hundred miles around might turn up some of
the pieces, which had fetched twenty or fifty or a hundred dollars or
more. But nobody in the pawn shop would remember who had sold
them. Some young man with a slightly bulbous head and dark hair.
Or was it a rather plain young woman with burning eyes?

ৰ্ক্ত ৰ্ক্ত

Kate thought a lot about her newly discovered talent for blackmail, but didn't tell Tom about it. Not yet. Not only was she withholding money from him, afraid he'd gamble it away, but now she withheld her thoughts. Tom was changing on her, and not for the good. The distance between them grew more out of him than from her.

The discovery came to her one day when she was dusting in a wealthy home in Chicago, and she spied a curious thing. Down the hall, in an alcove framed by bay windows, another young maid stood, also dusting. Thea was a modestly attractive girl of twenty. Kate knew of her, but had never exchanged more than a hello or goodbye with her. Thea did not appear to know Kate was watching from afar as the master of the house appeared behind her. He was a man of 50, a lawyer and partner in a big firm, with lots of money. His wife was an adorable blonde angel with beautiful blue eyes and a girlish mouth, and Kate could not imagine what her husband saw in other women. The master was not a handsome man at all, but a chubby toad with little short arms and no neck, who wore collars that rose to his ears. He had a wide, round head and was balding, and had fleshy lips that fairly reeked of his cheap appetites. His eyes fairly craned out on stalks in his hunger for forbidden fruits. His cultured wife, meanwhile, kept up a brave smile, and ushered their children through piano lessons, horseback riding, ballet, and other cultured skills, while her husband pursued depravities right under her roof.

As Kate watched, Thea kept dusting, but her pace changed. It was obvious she knew who was behind her, and what was coming next. The master came directly up behind her. He looked left and right but, in his impatience, he didn't see Kate watching from afar. He stood very close behind the girl for a few moments. She stopped dusting, and they seemed almost like one person. Kate watched him hand her a paper dollar, which she hid in her skirt. Then he stood behind her, feeling her body up and down. He handed her another bill, which she tucked away in an economy of motions. She leaned forward over a table. He lifted her skirts just enough, and pressed against her. He took her from behind in quick, rough, jerky motions. When he was done, he flung her hems down. He turned abruptly, without a smile or an endearment, buttoning his fly, and walked away as if he had just taken out the trash. Thea turned away to dab under her skirt with a cleaning cloth, and gradually resumed her work as if nothing had happened. Her expression, though unreadable even with Kate's sharp eyes, was not a pleased one. Kate loathed him, and formed a plan.

She crossed paths with him the very next day, in this household of a dozen or more women servants. Kate gave him her dazzling look, and the toad lit up. She waited for him in that very alcove, and he came up behind her. She took the dollar bill he offered, and let him feel under her dress. His hands trembled as his cold fingertips touched her warm skin. She almost choked with loathing as those chilly fingertips probed into ever more private places. He pressed another dollar on her for a minute's feeling.

This happened two or three times over the next few days. She kept the extra money from Tom. The toad became more and more enamored of her, so much so that she noticed the other maid shot her jealous looks. Finally, the toad showed her a twenty dollar bill and made sinuous motions and ravenous eyes—more mean-looking than seductive—as he blocked her into an alcove and pulled on her skirt. "Twenty I go all the way," he said. He licked his lips. She took the twenty and put it in her pocket. She took him by the lapel and swung him around. He grinned and looked happy as she pulled him around so she had him trapped in the corner with her hand still on his lapel. His leering smile vanished, replaced by a look of shock, as she spoke. "Now, buster, I have news for you. First of all, you're not getting any closer to me. Second, if I tell my husband, he'll come burn your house down and shoot you in the middle of the street like a dog. Third, I'm quitting this job right this minute, and you're going to hand me three hundred dollars cash or I go straight to your wife."

His expression went through a spectrum from shock to anger to contempt. He pushed her roughly away, though she was a half a head taller than him. "See here, bitch, how dare you talk to me like that?"

She shoved him back. "Don't try me, pal. You can either…"

He shoved her again and scoffed. "It's your word against mine. Who would believe a temporary domestic?"

"Try this on, you fool. Thea is willing to talk. Together, we can take you for twice as much." Thea knew nothing, but he wouldn't know that.

"You crooked scum." He showed snarling teeth and hateful eyes.

"You stupid, ugly old lecher. I have nothing to lose, but I can ruin you. Let's march straight to your office and get the cash, and I'm out the door."

"What if I tell the police?"

"Fine. Let's each tell our story. Your wife leaves you, and you're ruined. Come on, Frog Face, you've had your fun. Now pay up or else!"

She walked out of that house a quarter hour later with her three hundred dollars plus the twenty he'd given her initially. He would not tell his wife a thing, of that Kate was certain. He'd do as she told him, and tell his wife the temporary woman had quit, with many apologies, to care for her dying mother in—oh, make up a city, something new—Atlanta. She put the money aside where Tom wouldn't find it.

Kate found another position, and spent many hours working every week. She and Tom were having sex several times a week, but life with him was becoming joyless. She put a good face on things and tried to please him, but the lack of railroad work and a few gambling losses around town made him increasingly despondent. In that state, he grew more morose and violent, until sometimes she feared him.

Her other position came to an end, and she soon found a new one. She left every morning at dawn, and came tiredly trudging up the stairs every evening after dark, to find him either gone out gambling and drinking, or passed out with his head down among bottles on the kitchen table. She was thinking about giving him her extra money, just to please him. But there weren't that many toads in the world. She always kept enough of her earnings to buy food and pay the rent, and gave him the rest as he expected and demanded. She wished they were saving some, but it wasn't her place to tell him what to do.

Months went by, and Kate realized she had missed her period. She was throwing up every morning. Tom had been terrible lately, and she expected the wonderful news would turn things around. Maybe it was time to play the trains again. That seemed to keep Tom's spirits up and his mind focused. But she was tired of that life. They had run away from what was burned into her mind as that miserable, empty farm village of Washington, Iowa, with its long, desolate winters and inbred, narrow-minded religious bigots full of pretension and self-righteousness. Tom had been her soul-mate. It was he and she together against a world that did not understand their wild freedom. Tom and Kate loathed the little people who moved about in stolid, everyday gray little lives. She was running away, too, from the memory of her Eddie dying in that desolation during his second little day of life.

*E*ddie lay on his back in the crib, dressed in white, and waved his little hands fitfully like any baby. He seemed lusty at first, trying to stare up into the light with unseeing eyes the color of sea foam. His crying changed from energetic to a heartbroken little mewling, as if he knew something terrible was happening. How she held him, so close to her heart! He stopped crying. He wouldn't feed. By noon on the second day of his life, he not only grew silent in her desperate embrace, while she comforted him and begged him to stay, but he grew limp and cooled in her arms. She sobbed and shrieked and threw herself on the floor holding her dead baby. She raised him to her breast, and tried pushing a milk-dripping nipple into his mouth. Tom screamed and ran out of the house in terror and despair. A neighbor woman pried the lifeless, chill little body from her naked breast after a time, and what happened from there she would never rightly remember. It was all a nightmarish haze. Tom finally came and held her, for hours it seemed, and it was the closest they two had ever been.

Always the disapproving eyes of her wealthy grandfather floated in her memory when she thought of that horrific time. He had disowned Kate not long after, when it became clear she and Tom were not cut out do farming.

Now Kate and Tom were finally going to be mother and father again. As the changes flushed through her body, filling her with new life, she started thinking of maybe settling down—all sorts of weird thoughts she wasn't used to. A little house with a white picket fence in California. Why not? They couldn't live on the run forever. Surely Tom would see that.

Kate understood she was different in how she felt in her relationships with other people. She knew she did not have much feeling about other people. This made her cling to Tom all the more, because she loved him. She could watch Tom shoot a man dead and not blink an eye. But Eddie was the tragedy of her life, the one point where she felt like other mothers. She could never let go of the little baby's memory, but carried his image with her with an obsessive love that turned to anger and rage, and enabled her to hurt people like the toad-master without a moment's hesitation.

She never expected the reaction she got when she opened the door. Tom had been drinking heavily. She found him sitting at the kitchen table with his glass and bottle, staring into nowhere. "What's the matter, honey?" she said as she hung up her purse and bonnet. As he looked up at her, with a blank, lost gaze, she could not contain herself. She sat in his lap and put her arms around his head. "Darling, I have great news to tell you."

He looked up, his eyes blinking as if he'd been napping. "What?"

"We are going to be parents."

"What do you mean?"

She hugged him. "Things are going to be different."

His reaction surprised her. He seemed numb. She wondered if he had bought some heroin from the Chinese down the street. "What is the matter, darling? Aren't you happy? We're going to have another child."

He pulled her arms down from his neck. "I don't want to go through that again."

"Oh, honey, I understand how you feel. Our poor little Eddie..."

He pushed her away so that she almost fell, and rose. "Don't speak of him again!"

"He was your son, Tom." She stumbled against the table, bracing herself with both hands. This was entirely different than she had expected. "He is an angel in heaven, but he is still your son."

Tom was cool. "I can't stand this life anymore. I'm going to cage a pair of tickets so we can take the train across country. I've got the dark itch in my fingers, and I know I can get some money off those stupid guys. How are you going to work your end of it when your gut's hanging out there like a bag of oats?"

"Honey, we can't do that forever." Seeing the frustration in his eyes, she thought of giving him her money for his tickets. She had nearly four hundred dollars set aside. But she didn't want to do any more of that. She had not yet told her of the toad, and her plan to fleece more like him. "I can work as a domestic. You could take some little jobs here and there."

"Doing what?" Tom banged his fist on the table. "What's wrong with you? We live in this slum, and you want to raise children here?" He drew closer, so that she could smell tobacco and gin on his stained teeth. His eyes were red, and she could see the mixture of rage and worry in his features. His lower lip trembled. She felt sorry for him. She started to regret not taking precautions. Maybe she should get an abortion and wait for a better day. Maybe he was right. She didn't see him haul back.

Out of the blue, Tom's fist collided with her face, and she saw stars. From there on, it was all a blur. She went down, and he stood over her. She tried pleading with him as she lay on the dirty wooden floor that smelled faintly like railroad ties, but words would not come out. His boot landed in her side. At first he was not kicking her hard, just more or less rolling her over so he could slap her face back and forth with both palms. When she pulled her knees up to protect her stomach, and held her arms over her head, he yelled himself into an ever greater rage. She could not make out what he was yelling. At one point, when his face was close to her, and words exploded from his teeth, she punched him. He blinked stupidly and fell silent. She scrambled back and punched him again. He fell on his rear, sitting side-saddle on the floor holding his jaw with one hand and bracing himself behind with the other.

She staggered to her feet and ran. She made it as far as the back door. There, he tackled her. She had the door open and could feel the cold night air, which was a relief after the stuffy, smoky kitchen that stank of cabbage and puke. He hit her, like a bolt of lightning that made her stagger out onto the creaky wooden landing. As she held on to the stair rail with both hands, she saw in his eyes the utter lack of love or feelings for her and her condition. He kicked her, and she was dimly aware of rolling, banging her head, bouncing down the wooden stairs, head over heels—amid splintering wood and people exclaiming in horror nearby—into oblivion.

❦ ❦

Gradually, she woke into a hallucinatory state. The nausea and darkness told her, in caressing voices like nuns singing, that she was in the depths of an opium dream. Beyond that sphere of laudanum, she felt distant pain like broken furniture across a room. Her vision was blurry, and shadows moved around her. She smelled camphor and other pungent aromas, including the gnawing odor of hospital alcohol. Dimly, she thought she must still be alive, but something was badly broken and most of her body was utterly numb. She tried to signal to the shadows moving around her, but they had tied her hands and feet to the bed in which she lay, and she could not raise a hand though she tugged weakly. She could turn her head to look at her immoveable hand, and for a moment her near vision swam into focus so that she saw the hospital gauze with which they had bound her wrist to the bed post. But it was all a mystery to her, and she stared at her hand, and the wrist, and the gauze without being able to make sense of them. She tugged at the other hand, without looking, and it too seemed to be tied.

She heard a man sobbing in a nearby room, and voices comforting him. "My God, what has happened to her? She was just going out for some groceries, and I heard a terrible scream as she fell down the stairs."

A stern, older woman of authority said: "I am sorry she lost your baby, Mr. Morgan. If she lives, she will never be able to have children again."

❦ ❦

Kate awoke a long time later. Weeks had passed. The pain, the withdrawal from opium, had all passed. Miraculously, she had not suffered any broken bones. She sat in a high-backed wicker wheel chair with great big-spoked wheels with rubber tires. Someone had dressed her in a flannel gown, and a blanket lay across her lap. She was alone in a quiet solarium overlooking a green lawn, and the city skyline loomed beyond that in glorious sunshine. She called out, and when nobody came, she threw the blanket aside and tried to stand up. Her legs would not obey, and she uttered a convulsive scream. *Paralyzed!* In terror, she gripped the table beside her and pulled herself erect, falling on the cold floor as she did so. Sobbing, she crawled away from the wheel chair. Two nurses with white nunnish wimples came running. "Mrs. Morgan! You've fallen from your chair!" said one. They helped her to her feet.

"Am I paralyzed?"

"Why no," said the other. "You're weak from weeks lying in bed."

Kate, over the next few days, tested her legs—first one, then the other, and kept alternating, lifting them, feeling her rubbery muscles—but she was determined to get out of here, to start walking, to run for miles and miles and get her strength back.

"We thought we were going to lose you a few times."

"You had a terrible infection, and you know—" They both looked at her sadly. "You lost the baby. And you won't be able to have any more."

Kate remembered all the things she had overheard, and fell back into the wheelchair sobbing. She cried her heart out, and the two women left her alone.

Within a few days, still feeling the tiniest bit weak, but almost back to her normal self, Kate Morgan stood in the lobby of the hospital with her bag. A nun had walked her out; had brought her bag along and set it on the floor. The nun handed her something, saying: "They brought this in with you— it fell off you when you went down the steps."

It was her gold locket, which contained her only picture of her lost child Eddie. The nuns said they were expecting Tom would come to pick her up, as he had promised someone he would. Kate looked at herself in a mirror as she put her locket back on, by its fine little gold chain. She looked gaunt, with big hollow eyes and protruding cheekbones. Her sense of loss radiated from those eyes. Twice now she had lost that precious gift, and now it would never come again. It was something she could not forgive Tom for—not this. Anything else, but not taking that away. Most women had many children, and lost a few along the way. It was normal, even though it hurt terribly. You never forgot that brief, tiny life you would have loved to nurture into a strapping son or daughter. Now she had this to bear, and she would bear it for the rest of her life. She had always dreamed of one day leading a normal life somewhere, once her demons had their fill and left her, but now she was resigned to being a shadow of a woman. She determined she could not be at the whim of the destroyer any longer. Gathering her shawl around her, and picking up her satchel, she made her way slowly and effortfully out the door.

On the great steps overlooking the city, she was overwhelmed by the noise and the colors and the thousands of bustling people, carts, horses with clattering hooves, rumbling electric trolleys, billboards, smoking locomotives, and yelling vendors. The smell of horse manure and men's cigars and a thousand things burning, rotting, flowering, decaying, almost made her want to return to the green and silent womb of the hospital. But she pushed that morbid thought away.

To hell with Tom Morgan. To hell with her grandfather, the wealthy and stern miller back in Iowa. To hell with the toads and grabbers of this world. She had a life to live, and she would make the most of it in whatever way was hers to make it work. As she walked back to the tenements, she picked up her step. Her legs seemed to grow stronger, and the warm spring city air filled her lungs. She was 24 years old, and by God she was determined to enjoy her youth to the fullest. She resisted the urge to feel sorry for herself.

The tenements were noisy and smelly as ever. She hoped Tom wasn't there. Looking up, she saw the place seemed dark, as if nobody were home. She had only one errand here, and that was to pick up her belongings. Then she would disappear where Tom could never find her.

As she walked up the outside steps in back, she was surrounded by blurry, running, yelling children. She almost welcomed their noise in her ears. It was the music of life. She climbed up the wooden stairs to the third floor landing, from which Tom had kicked her. Someone had replaced several broken pieces of the railing. The apartment window was dark. As she turned the key in the lock and opened the door, her heart froze.

There, sitting at the table amid a litter of empty liquor bottles, was Tom Morgan, smoking. His eyes were red from drink, and he had a cold cigar butt in one dirty yellow hand. He had not washed or shaved in a week or more, from the looks of him. When he saw her, he stumbled to his feet so the wooden chair fell over backwards. "Katie, my love…"

"I have nothing to say to you."

He fell to his knees on the floor and raised his coupled hands in prayer. "My darling, my wife, I beg you, forgive me for what I have done."

"You are not the boy I fell in love with back in Iowa." She walked past him and pulled her trunk from under the bed. Surprised at her own furious strength, she sat it open on the bed and added her belongings on top of those already in the trunk—including one of Eddie that she prized above all, a wispy lock of her lost son's hair.

Tom knelt behind her and wrapped his arms around her thighs. "Katie, my darling, I can't live without you."

She struggled to get free. She waved the lock of Eddie's hair and yelled: "This one at least I have something to remember him by. The one you just killed I don't even know if it was a boy or a girl. Get away from me." She smashed her hand across his mouth and nose, and he sat back holding his face. A noose bleed shot between his fingers. He got that ominous fury in his eyes as he rose and walked to the stove, where he rattled the empty kettle and tossed it aside, then to the sink. They had only cold water, when that was running, and there wasn't time to heat water on the stove. Cold water was just right for stopping a bloody nose. She could see the violence building in him, and yelled: "So, you dirty bastard, you want to finish the job and kill me while you still can? Because I'm leaving you, and there is nothing you can do or say to keep me with you. You don't deserve a wife. You don't even deserve a dog that you can beat and kick around."

"Katie, my love, think of our years together." He held a cold, wet towel to his face and turned, looking exhausted. "I'm sorry, Katie, I'll make it up to you, I swear."

"How can you make it up to me?" she yelled as she gathered her coat and hat and a few other belongings and threw them in the trunk. She walked to the door, stepped out onto the landing, and yelled down to the unemployed men milling below around a whiskey bottle. "I need a man to carry my trunk. Give you a quarter." There was a rumble of feet as they fought to climb over each other, up the stairs, and she pointed to one she knew, Magruder, a big quiet reliable man. "You'll get the trunk for me, and I'll tell you where to bring it when we're gone from here."

Magruder trudged up the steps, eyeballing Tom Morgan nervously. He wore a gray woolen slouch hat and a rumpled gray suit stained with sweat from many days' work when there had been work to do. He could probably hold his own against the whipcrack Morgan, but he wasn't a man who relished a fight. With his missing teeth, he kept nervously chewing his tongue and flicking its pink serpentine length among his various stumps like an eel underwater. He walked with his fists balled, keeping a nervous gaze on Tom Morgan, who stood dabbing himself on the face with the rose-stained towel.

Kate told him: "Go on, take the trunk down and I'll be after you in a minute." Ignoring Tom, she looked about to make sure she had not forgotten anything. Tom didn't get in Magruder's way—clearly that was not the fight Tom wanted to pick just now. Magruder left with the trunk, clomping down the wooden stairs. The noise of children, the wind, the city clamor, rose up as he went down. Kate turned and started for the door, but Tom blocked it. "Katie, you're my wife. I forbid you to leave."

"You can't stop me, Tom. Don't even try."

Tom closed the door, so that they were alone and shut in. "Kate, you've had your say, and now I'll have mine."

She started around him, but he gripped her arm in a steely hand. As she struggled to escape, he yanked her back. He gripped both her arms, and she cried out in pain. He reeked sourly of whiskey, and his breath was foul from sore gums and unbrushed teeth stained with cigar juice. "Kate, Kate, stop it, Kate, Kate," he said in a low, warning voice that usually meant kicks and blows were coming.

"You've already killed me," she wailed. "What more can you do but kick my poor body to death?"

"I'm not going to do anything bad to you," he slurred. But his grip on her was like a vise. She tried to wriggle free, and he dug his thumbs painfully into the nerves above the hollows of her elbows. She started to cry with pain. He pressed her toward the bed, speaking in that low, ominous voice: "Katie...Katie...look at me...I can't live without you..." He threw her down on the bed, and then stood undoing his belt. For a moment she thought he was going to rape her. But the belt came off, and the square steel buckle dangled at his knees like a weapon. "I'll kill you before I let you leave me."

Still rubbing the numbness in each arm where he had gripped her, she rolled out of the way as the belt descended on the bed. The steel buckle landed with a thump in the pillow beside her skull. With a choking shriek of terror, she rolled off the bed and into the narrow space between bed and wall, onto the dusty, dirty wooden floor. Tom started to climb over the bed. Raising her feet, with her back propped against the wall, she shoved the flimsy steel bed against him. He yelled in pain as it gouged his shins. "Damn you, woman! Just trying to reason with you. Now you're in for it!"

One of his Deringers lay on the floor in a heap of soiled clothing. She reached behind to get to the gun, sprawling awkwardly. He came crawling around the bed and grabbed her ankle. She kicked him in the head with her free foot, but he was unstoppable. She saw his full rage and fury come to the fore, clouded by days of drinking, and she hoped there was a round in the chamber as she aimed the gun at his face and pressed the trigger.

At that very moment, he jerked on her leg, and the shot went off a bit, creating a red splash in his filthy gray shirt, halfway between his neck and his shoulder joint. He grimaced, and gripped the wound.

She pulled the trigger again, but nothing more came out. She remembered it was a single-shooter. She dropped the gun, kicked him in the face with her free foot, and struggled up over the bed. He pushed himself up along the wall and started after her. She picked up the belt that lay on the floor, held it in both hands, and swung it fully around as hard as she could. She heard the crack as it connected with his head, and he went down like a sack. She stumbled to the door, sobbing, yanked it open, and ran outside without looking back or shutting the door. She half ran, half staggered down the stairs, one flight after another, until she arrived in the courtyard. The men standing around, amid a thousand yelling and running little street Arabs, were used to fights and screams and looked at her dumbly.

Magruder stood by the trunk, tipped his hat, and his eelish tongue ran a few pink flicks amid the yellow reefs of his mouth.

Shortly, Kate and Magruder were on their way down the dirt alley. She held his quarter, and he carried her trunk on his shoulder as if he were an elephant of a man. Tom appeared on the balustrade high above, clutching his nicked shoulder. Streams of blood crisscrossed each other on his face from the wound on his head. "Kate, don't leave me! Please! I love you." She ignored him. Men all around sniggered, because none liked Morgan. Tom yelled all the louder: "You are my wife! I will find you, woman. Look over your shoulder every day! You are mine, and I will have you back no matter where you go." Then he could be heard brokenly wailing in his drunken state, both from his physical pain and from the loss of her as Kate walked out of his life. She would keep looking over her shoulder for the rest of her life, but now she began to think about where her path would take her next.

2. Lizzie & John–Late Summer 1892

The city of Detroit loomed large and industrial and dotted with lights as dusk fell on a hot summer afternoon. The city's downtown streets were jammed with horses, buggies, and street cars. Pedestrians in fine clothing were out for a refreshing stroll as the evening breeze replaced the sullen humidity of day. Shop windows were brightly lit and stuffed full of goods. Above the windows were endless competing signs and billboards, some twinkling with myriad little metallic disks, others with flashing colored lights. Theater marquees shone brightly. Ticket booths stayed busy as men and women lined up to buy seats.

An attractive young couple hurried along, dressed in their finest. They held hands and half ran, half walked toward a performance of Denman Thompson's popular comedy, *The Old Homestead*. The girl was Elizabeth 'Lizzie' Wyllie, aged 24, and she loved theater. Her eyes were bright with excitement. Her smile was dazzling as she looked up at her companion with love, and held hands with him. Lizzie was a beautiful young woman, always elegant in her manner and dress, and people turned their heads to look after her. Her lover was John Longfield, a good-looking tall dark-haired man with a rakish twinkle in his eye, dimpled cheeks, and a card-player's deceptive grin under a pencil mustache. He said to her "Come on, Lizzie, we'll go in the side entrance. I got tickets from my friend Steve."

Lizzie loved him and his take-charge manner. John seemed to know his way around people and situations, whereas she was—to begin with—near sighted, and on top of that not terribly good at reading people or understanding how to finagle things the way John always did. What would not be apparent to the casual eye, either, was that she was a single girl and he was a married man. In fact, he was her foreman at a large Detroit bookbindery. It wasn't clear to her whether his wife knew what he did, and she could never get him to quite spell things out about that or about their relationship. They had fallen into a mad, passionate sexual love affair a few months ago—Spring 1892—and had begun to attract attention in the work place. Lizzie's sister May, the sensible sibling, also worked there and kept telling Lizzie to be prudent and to be discreet. As far as Lizzie was concerned, she had been lonely and unhappy for some time, and she hoped...well, she knew it would be a bad thing to wish that he'd leave his wife and children for her. She'd never met the wife, but sort of pictured her as a dumpy workhorse who was afraid to stand in his way for fear of losing him and the household income. In this world, a woman alone, with children, abandoned by her husband, was at best an object of pity—what had she done to drive him away? What was wrong with her? At worst, one might speculate that perhaps she had been caught in some indecent situation and he had, in his justifiable outrage, moved away to maintain his honor and integrity in the eyes of society. Then again, plenty of people were practical and realistic, and realized that men were like the wolf or any other opportunistic predator, so the woman should not always be blamed. Lizzie was willing to settle for being his mistress, if only he would set her up in a little place of her own so she wouldn't have to live with her loving but impossibly domineering mother any longer, and share a bedroom with her loving but strong-willed sister May. All these thoughts, and the dark blot of bad memories about her previous misadventure in sex, formed a blurred and fleeting background to her sense of pleasure as she ran along the sidewalk with John. Steve could have been John's twin, complete with mustache and rakish grin, as he opened a side door and let them in. John handed him something—money, Lizzie thought—and Steve solicitously escorted them through a door, to a winding little stairwell that led up to good seats in the mezzanine.

For the next few hours, Lizzie laughed and clapped delightedly, while John kept his arm around her and absently fondled her in the dark. Sometimes, she responded by touching him. It excited her that he seemed to always be erect around her, and that made her feel hot inside. She had learned that if she let him go too far, or too long, or if she responded too ardently in these public situations, then he would lose some of that cool veneer and become too heated. That in turn might attract attention from others in the seats around them, and that would mortify Lizzie—because she was by nature always lady-like, demure, and cool. It wasn't that she was putting on an act. She was just naturally dignified like that, and people often thought she was wealthy. She had long ago accepted who she was—a myopic, beautiful factory girl with champagne tastes and a beer pocket book, as one of her old *beaux* used to say. She had always assumed one day a boy with some style and money would take a fancy to her, and she'd live in a big house with servants. In the meantime, she was quite content to go out with May now and then for a beer at the German gardens, or a walk in the Campus Martius with John. She knew nobody would approve of her relationship with her foreman, so she had kept the affair a secret. If the women at work were beginning to notice, well, so what? As long as she and John were discreet, nobody would get hurt or embarrassed. Her happy, cozy affair could play out in its own little world.

Lizzie had seen this production a dozen times, and knew its main acts by heart. The piece was a record-breaking success around the country—the story of a New England rustic who leaves his village for the big city, has many misadventures, and is only too happy to return to his simple life. The play plucked nerve strings around the nation, but Lizzie especially appreciated its sentimentality. And she had a rare eye for fine costume.

John arranged for her to meet one of the stars at a reception in the lobby afterward. About a hundred men and women crowded around for punch and snacks. The noise seemed deafening and overwhelming to Lizzie, who still felt tender with the story's magic. Actors and actresses, still in stage costume, mingled with guests. John said: "Lizzie, over here, quick, I want you to meet someone." John led a spellbound Lizzie toward Steve, who stood waiting beside a splendid actress in beautiful white gown and large silvery wig. She did not seem entirely comfortable. Steve said: "Oh, hello John—Lizzie—please meet Miss Lilly."

Lizzie said "The famous actress!" and Miss Lilly brightened.

John said to Miss Lilly: "My lady friend and I have been dying to speak with you. We enjoy your performances so much—we've seen you three times so far."

Miss Lilly said: "Why thank you. That's so nice to hear. What a beautiful young lady!"

Lizzie said: "Thank you! Your dress is absolutely fabulous. You must have a great designer and tailor to do such fine work."

Miss Lilly said: "I do, my dear. You're not only a theater fan, but a *connoisseuse* of fine dress. Are you an actress also?"

Lizzie said: "No, hardly. I have wicked stage fright, and can never remember any lines. I was thrown out of my second grade school play because I couldn't remember some dumb lines about a rabbit." Miss Lilly's dazzling features grew confused—Lizzie was not the person she'd been told she would be seeing.

John, aside, asked Steve: "Can you get me the tickets I asked about?"

Steve said: "We'll see what I can do about those tickets. Will you be stopping by the office anytime soon? I'll be waiting for you."

John said: "You'll see plenty of me."

Miss Lilly said: "I see my manager over there. I must leave you. It was such a pleasure to chat with you all. Bye!"

❧ ☙

On the way home, John and Lizzie ambled happily under the gas lamps on the street. Both lived in central Detroit. He would put her on a streetcar, and then take a different car to his home about a mile away. "I have a present for you."

"What is it?" They stopped under a street light. He held out a little box. She opened it and gasped. On a bed of cotton lay two pretty silver earrings. "John, these are beautiful." She kissed him on the lips, briefly and excitedly, before returning her wide-eyed and open mouthed attention to the earrings. "I'll have to get my ears pierced finally."

He held one up, and she obliged by turning her head to one side with a happy look. "They will look gorgeous on you."

"Thank you so much!" Lizzie said. She put the box in her purse, and they continued walking arm in arm. "What a thrilling evening."

John said: "One of these days, darling, you'll win the lottery or I'll hit it big at cards, and we'll have a nest egg."

Lizzie clung to him. "That's a lovely dream, John. I love when you take me to the theater, and to such splendid parties."

John said: "You are a lady of class, sweetheart. I am proud to be seen with you. "

Lizzie beamed and said: "Until the dream comes true, I just want to take things a moment at a time, savor the good, and put up with our poor, everyday lives as we are." She put her hand against his heart and gave him a dazzling smile. "One day, we'll belong just to each other, won't we?"

John put his hand over hers, holding it to his heart, and regarded her with unknown calculations in his eyes, saying nothing.

Not long after the theater night, Lizzie and her mother, Elizabeth Wyllie, and her sister May were in their kitchen at home. Late summer sunshine poured in through the one small window with its gray sheer curtains. It was humble, but cozy—it was all the home the three women knew, and a loving one at that.

May sat in her corner, rattling away at her sewing machine while her foot pumped underneath. Lizzie lay curled up with a book on the sofa. She wore eyeglasses and read her novel with a serious expression.

Mrs. Wyllie carefully took a hot baking sheet from the oven. "Here you go, girls, for your day off. Fudge brownies with powder sugar." She regarded Lizzie and chided lovingly: "Now she is wearing her glasses for a change. What vanity—only when she reads her fantasies."

May said: "Nose stuck in a book as usual. What are you reading, bookworm sister?"

Lizzie looked up from her book as if in a great trance. "What?"

May said: "What tragedy of love and death are you devouring?"

Lizzie said: "The newest novel by the English author Thomas Hardy. It was published last year. It's about this beautiful maiden, and titled *Tess D'Urberville, A Pure Woman Faithfully Presented*, who started out pure, but was brought low by a careless man, and the evil world in general." Lizzie sighed, shuddered, and hugged her book. "I'm almost done. What a dreamy feeling. I could just die with Tess, or I could cry all day."

May said: "I know what you mean. What is it about love sorrow that makes us weepy and we can't get enough of all that sentiment?"

Mrs. Wyllie served cookies with a pleased look, though she pretended to be grumpy. "Two young girls looking for the loves of your lives. Beautiful flowers, waiting for just the right butterfly. Watch that you don't land some handsome moth in a cheap suit, singing you lines written in heaven with the devil's own pen."

Lizzie laughed. "You mean, wearing cheap wings." She and May laughed, and even their mother cracked a reluctant grin. May said to Lizzie: "I don't read like you do, but I adore those theater plays. Like Dickens' tragic Little Nell—a fallen angel."

Mrs. Willey said: "You girls have your heads in the clouds. You're a bright girl, Lizzie, and with all your reading you could have gone to teacher's school."

May said: "Must you bring that up again, Mom?"

Lizzie said: "At my age, it's too late now. What a terrible thing that was. I would still never let a man see me with eyeglasses!" She closed her eyes and reflected back on that day of anguish.

∾ ∾

It had happened a few years ago at the teachers' college entrance exam. A young, bookish Lizzie, wearing glasses, stood among ninety other girls awaiting admission to the test hall. The corridor had that forbidding shine, and a severe wax smell, that always reminded Lizzie of those dreadful tests she rarely ever passed. Her mother had made her come here, and she was sure she would fail. Just because she was bookish didn't mean she was teacher material—Lizzie knew that, but her mother needed to have it demonstrated. Nearby stood a hundred or more boys waiting to be admitted by another door. Beyond was a single large room, with the girls' exam desks on one side, and the boys' exam desks on the other side, separated by a wide aisle.

Seeing the boys outside—as the boys and girls exchanged shy, interested looks—Lizzie furtively put her glasses away and fluffed her hair.

A bell shrilled. The doors burst open.

The exam candidates poured into the room and took their seats.

On the blackboard were the rules, clearly written, among them: *No satchels, books, or notes of any kind.*

All the other students left their satchels on the floor by the back wall.

Lizzie, who couldn't read the board, walked in and sat down, putting her satchel under her chair. Soon, the exams began.

Students were bent over their test booklets in deep and stressful concentration. Stern and scary proctors marched about like police detectives in black suits.

Lizzie was working hard on her exam.

Suddenly, a proctor pointed from a distance—at Lizzie's satchel under the chair. She was reaching down for a hankie to blow her nose. Several proctors hurried to her desk. They took her exam book away, and escorted a shocked and tearful Lizzie from the exam hall. She never did try to take the exam again, but found work, along with her sister, at Winn and Hammond Bookbinders.

In the kitchen today with Lizzie and May, a few years later, Mrs. Wyllie said: "We all make mistakes. Life goes on. Vanity is one of the deadly sins or is it? We will be okay, we three, if we stick together, work hard, and stay out of trouble."

Mrs. Wyllie left the room with a load of wash.

Lizzie said: "I heard that our American Stephen Crane is working on a book titled *Maggie: A Girl of the Streets*. I can't wait to read it."

May said: "I just love those tragedies. Let me know if you hear of a good play. "

Lizzie said: "I have a gentleman friend who has good taste in theater, and he'll take me. Maybe he'll bring you too."

May said: "Do I know this gentleman friend?"

Lizzie shrugged her shoulders and smiled secretively. "I can't tell."

May said: "Oh no, Lizzie, I know who it is. Don't go with him. He's bad news."

About that same time of year, late summer, John Longfield and Lizzie Wyllie walked arm in arm on gravel walks amid flowered lawns, to the tunes of distant calliope music. There was a carnival in a far corner of the park, with music and rides.

John and Lizzie stopped to smell gorgeous, colorful flowers.

Women with parasols and men in straw boater hats strolled by.

John bought Lizzie a cotton candy.

Lizzie was joyful as John helped her on a carnival ride. She had already dismissed the cautions uttered by her sister, and she had sworn May to secrecy. If her mother ever found out—there would be the dickens to pay, because Lizzie had already once made a terrible mistake of this nature, and it didn't seem possible that she would fall into the same ditch again. But, looking back on it all some months later, half a continent away, in a fairy-tale hotel and resort overlooking a stunning vista of Pacific Ocean and Coronado Beach and Cabrillo Point, Lizzie would have occasion to ponder the collision course on which she already was, unwittingly, during those innocent strolls in the park.

જ ન

The factory hall was gloomy, with dusty air illumined through barred, jail-like windows. The hall was full of women of all ages engaged in the complex stages of case binding, from gathering the signatures to folding and stitching them on wooden frames, and building the covers around them. May and Lizzie were busy at a bench with eight other women.

A door across the floor, marked *Foreman*, opened, and John Longfield peered out.

May looked up, and caught Longfield's hungry look toward Lizzie.

Longfield closed the door.

May watched her sister rise. Lizzie wiped her hands on a cloth, and walked off to the ladies' room. Minutes later, she was on her way back. All the women noticed.

Lizzie knocked on the foreman's door. The door opened, revealing a brief glimpse of Longfield. Lizzie entered the room. The door closed, and the women at the bench with May exchanged looks. Some were darkly amused, others scandalized.

જ ન

Inside the office, Longfield's naked back moved in sensual thrusting motions over a long table. Under him, Lizzie's ecstatic face looked up, enraptured. Her eyes opened and closed with each of his long, slow strokes, except to flicker now and then, to look up at him with love and ardor.

Lizzie got on top, riding him, swaying sensuously. Longfield clasped her buttocks as he thrust upward, again and again and again.

Lizzie said: "John, John, I love you so."

John said: "And I adore you, Lizzie, my darling."

Lizzie said: "Promise you'll keep me forever!"

John did not answer, but he grunted as he approached climax, and his rutting drowned out any reply he might have made.

John Longfield was one of several men playing cards at a round table in a dark, smoky den. It was in the cellar of a cheap hotel downtown. The bare stone walls had been white-washed. Only a few narrow slit-windows near the ceilings let out smoke and brought in fresh air.

A stony-faced waiter in a long white apron brought the men round after round of tall beers dripping with foam.

In the background, a crippled man with an eye patch fiddled a lilting sea chantey. A hat sat at his feet with change in it. A few bar flies hung about—older women with leathery skin and missing teeth.

The card game was hard and spirited.

John Longfield happened to be on a lucky streak. He cleaned out an angry, puffy-faced man. The loser reluctantly paid up in the form of a tin money clip with several bills folded into it, which he tossed on the table as he stormed out.

In a dirty alley full of puddles and horse droppings, against the backdrop of a brick factory wall and an open gate where a horse-drawn delivery cart came rumbling out, Steve had his 'office,' as he called it. He was perennially one step ahead of the vice squad, several of whom were on his payroll and would tip him off about raids. Steve worked as a pimp, cardsharp, drug dealer, petty thief, and burglar—at the moment hanging out with three of his prostitutes.

A regular with a white mustache came down the street. He wore a black suit and bowler hat, and had a black umbrella over one arm. Names were never part of the transaction. The man never came within view under a street lamp, but stopped some distance away and pointed to one of the women. She nodded and hurried toward the man, giving raunchy come-on gestures to get him going and make it quick. The two disappeared into the shadows together, arm in arm.

John Longfield appeared. Steve walked away from his two women to meet him. Longfield pulled out the tin money clip with the bills. "Here it is, like I promised. For the earrings and the tickets, and Miss Lilly."

Steve rattled a finger over the bills as if counting. He pocketed them. "Perfect. Did she like the earrings?"

"She was ecstatic." Steve was also a fence for burglars. Lizzie did not ever need to know her expensive earrings came from a wealthy home across the city. "Thanks."

"Any time I can be of service, Johnny Boy."

John said: "You did fine. My little Lizzie loves nice clothes and jewelry. And she loves anything to do with theater. Getting Miss Lilly out there was an accomplishment."

"The timing was good. I told her I am a press agent, and a critic wanted to talk with her. Instead, you showed up with your girl. I think she got a little confused, expecting you to ask for an interview. No matter. Was your girlfriend pleased?"

"It went off perfectly," John said: "I need to keep it going. She loves me, and I do have a soft spot for the little thing."

"She's a beauty. You're a lucky man. I can arrange something else soon. How about balcony tickets for a nice romantic play?"

John said: " She'd love it!"

"Consider it done. I'll need some extra by Tuesday."

☙   ❧

On a hot summer day, Lizzie and May walked along a sidewalk on their way to work. The young women stayed under the shade of awnings as much as the could. The sidewalk glittered under their feet, all concrete and silica, hot enough to fry an egg.

May said: "You really mustn't see him, Lizzie."

Lizzie said: "But he makes me so dreamy."

May said: "Don't you ever learn? Don't you remember what happened when you were eighteen? "

Lizzie said: "But this is different. John may seem rough until you know him. He has such good taste in clothing, theater, all the nice things in life."

❧   ❧

That evening, Mrs. Wyllie was doing dishes in her kitchen. May sat in the corner at her sewing machine. Lizzie opened the door and came happily into the apartment. "Good evening!"

May froze over her sewing, and looked on darkly. Elizabeth sniffed Lizzie's breath: "Lizzie, where have you been? I smell gin, girl."

Lizzie said: "Oh, Mommy..." She started washing her hands at the sink.

Elizabeth grabbed her daughter roughly by the shoulders. "You're smoked like a sausage. You've been with men—wrong side of the tracks, by the smell of those cheap stogies."

Lizzie said: "Mother! I am 24 years old and a grown woman. It's summer, and I want to live a little."

Her mother said: "I hear you're seeing a married man."

"Not true!"

Mother put a hand on Lizzie's shoulder. "Lizzie, don't lie to me."

Lizzie shrieked: "May, you traitor!"

May shook her head and looked on silently.

Elizabeth said: "Lizzie, you dim thing! Don't you remember the hell you put us through? How you suffered? Having it and giving it up like that?"

Lizzie said: "Mind your own business, Mommy!"

Elizabeth said: "As long as you live under my roof, what you do is my business. I want no scandal in my home."

Lizzie said: "Then I'll leave!"

"Where would you go, poor factory girl who thinks she's an actress?"

Lizzie said: "Grand Rapids, for one thing."

"To my sister? You think she'd take you in?"

Lizzie said: "I'm just saying. Aunt Louisa is calm and understanding."

"Louisa Anderson has not been through the devil and back with you. She doesn't know the half."

3. Kate Morgan–Late Summer 1892

In a tiny room, on a morning in late summer 1892, Kate Morgan sat on her neatly made bed, with her head bowed and her hands raised. She stared at her palms, holding her locket on a fine chain.

The room was stripped of her personal possessions. She wore street clothing. Her maid's uniform was stuffed in her open satchel, and a distinctive wooden trunk stood closed nearby with a sense of finality and transition. It was the same trunk Magruder had carried down the stairs nearly four years earlier, the day she had last seen Tom in Chicago. She had moved around to many cities, plying her trade, and staying one step ahead of the shadowy husband she feared might still be tracking her.

Her face looked pale and transfigured as if she were staring into another world. The atmosphere around her, by contrast, was dark and brooding, filled with danger. But she was used to that. It was part of her way of living and surviving. What she could never get used to was the truth and finality of what she was staring at—her past, and its breaking point.

Kate looked unutterably sad and vulnerable in that moment.

Outside the dark little bubble of her moment, had she looked up at her two windows, she would have seen a sweeping view of the city in summer bloom. Her employer's house stood atop a hill, and a good part of the best of glorious San Francisco spread before her, including the cliffs that opened like a doorway to the Pacific Ocean.

In San Francisco Bay, the harbor still bristled with a forest of ships' masts, but a number of new steam ships showed their funnels among them.

The hills were covered with houses and tree crowns, all choked in fragrant blossoms. In the distance stood the Spreckels mansion at Washington and Van Ness Streets, among smaller but fine homes. The Spreckels family, whose patriarch was the so-called Hawai'ian sugar baron, Claus Spreckels, controlled much of the Pacific sugar industry. They owned vast holdings of cane fields under the Kalakaua Dynasty. Kate's boss was an executive in Spreckels' sugar industries, and owned this beautiful home with two dozen servants on Nob Hill.

This room would be her bedroom no longer. Kate Morgan heard footsteps approach. She heard the voice of Ida, the chief of female domestic staff, who was subordinate only to the butler. Kate pictured Ida in a long black uniform dress and white starched cap as she walked down a carpeted corridor in the maids' quarters. A heavier set of footfalls rumbled along with her—a porter wearing hobnail boots. The two stopped at Kate's door, and the rumbling ceased. Ida knocked imperiously.

Kate ignored the knocks as she sat on her bed and stared into the locket.

Ida said: "You're wanted downstairs."

Kate said icily: "I'll be out in a moment" She stared longingly at a tiny portrait. The newborn infant's eyes had a glazed look. The image was bordered in mourning black—a Victorian death photograph. Kate whispered: "Eddie." She closed the locket.

Ida rapped loudly. "You better not keep the boss waiting!"

Kate held the locket in her fist for a long moment as she closed her eyes with intense concentration.

Ida pounded on the door. "I don't have time for this."

Kate rose, assuming a stony look. Her world was as big as that locket, as big as her trunk, as small as this cramped room that had been her home—no, her place to collapse in exhaustion after a day's unrelenting work—for several weeks. As the pounding continued, she opened her eyes and saw herself in the mirror above the wash basin—a glowering, plain woman with cunning eyes, a fearless expression, and a full mouth. And what she wanted was what she was talented at extracting money from her employers. The moment had come again. She ignored Ida and clutched her locket a moment longer—as if it contained her very heart locked up in its cold metal casing.

Kate snapped the door open and stepped out, holding her satchel. Instantly, she was in charge, just by her demeanor. She regarded the domestic with a smoldering, wounded, threatening intensity that signaled Kate felt she had nothing to lose, and was capable of anything. The older woman stepped back, blanching, and spoke in a faint and tremulous voice. Her eyes were wide, and her rudeness was gone. "Claire, the boss wants to see you in his study." Kate knew the woman had no idea why the boss wanted to see her, and walked past her as if she were an insect.

The porter stood apologetically behind Kate, eyeballing her room over her shoulder, and the object he'd been sent to fetch. Kate told him over her shoulder, without looking back: "Wait for me outside by the curb. I won't be long."

"Yes, Miss Claire." Kate heard him tromp into the room to lift her wooden trunk. Ida scurried inside, with a wide-eyed afterglance, to start fluffing the bed, which Kate had perfectly made and needed no fluffing.

As Kate walked away from her room, down a maze of carpeted hallways with oak wainscoting and leaded glass windows, she spotted someone out of the corner of her eye. Emily, a fellow domestic, stood far down a cross hall. Kate knew very little of her—only that Emily had a reputation for being an impoverished, childless widow, who lived in a seedy neighborhood and drank herself into a stupor every night. Emily gave Kate a strange, meaningful look and an odd, unholy grin. Kate wondered—did Emily know? Was she a threat? There was something loaded and dangerous about Emily's hard face.

They were alone in the room together—Kate, and her employer. In the smoky, mahogany gloom of a richly appointed library, the boss stood stiffly behind his desk. Books were all around on the walls, Oriental carpets on the floors, vases, umbrellas, top hats of the upper society, all sorts of knick-knacks, many of them quite expensive. Standing before him was Kate in her street clothes, with her satchel on the floor.

The boss, a fastidious, well dressed man, said: "Damn you!"

Kate said: "No, damn yourself. You mistook an innocent smile for a young woman's careless flirtation, and pressed yourself upon me with gross physicality."

The boss said: "Oh, what nonsense. You offered yourself, and I had a moment of mental and moral weakness. I thought that somehow I could find pleasure in your carnality."

Kate said: "You'd better watch your mouth, you impertinent pecker-head. Who do you think you are, talking to a woman that way?"

Boss said: "Okay, okay—I'm sorry. Please—Miss Lomax—take your pay and go away."

Kate said: "I'll spare your wife and children the embarrassment of a public disgrace, you sanctimonious pig. Pay me my quitting wage plus three hundred, and we'll be done."

He had been ready for this. He counted out twenties with a cynical, defeated grin. He said: "Is your name really even Claire Lomax?"

Kate said: "Lay it to rest." She pocketed the money.

He stood uncomfortably, perhaps thinking of going to the police.

She walked to the door, stopped half way, and turned. She said: "Forget your pecker pride, and think of your family. Three hundred dollars is a small price to pay, rather than go to the police and have the whole city laughing at you and you lose your job, your house, your family. Think carefully." She had a last glimpse of the boss. He stood scared and sweaty in place for a long moment, and wiped a trembling hand across his brow. It was a scenario Kate had engineered often enough by now. This one had gone well. Served him right.

She slammed the door shut and strode down the hall. Her young, robust body moved with a seductive, hippy fullness that no employer with meandering eyes could miss under the dark dress. Her secret weapon was a subliminal, sensual allure that she broadcast with all her charm and guile. She was not beautiful—some might think her plain—but she was a dark-haired destroyer with fierce eyes and imposing, intelligent features.

She'd seen the look on Emily's face in that corridor, signaling some dark intention. Outside, Kate again saw Emily's pale face floating behind an upper story stairwell window. Kate tipped the porter and climbed aboard the Stanhope—a horse-drawn, open buggy with an accordion-top folded up—on whose rear boot the porter had loaded her trunk.

🙰 🙵

In the gloom of a tavern—which smelled richly of beer, bread, and meat, as well as coffee and cigar smoke—Kate sipped at a mug of beer as she sat in a corner reserved for the female gender. She ate a corned beef sandwich with a gherkin on the side. She was flush, on vacation, and feeling good. She wore traveling clothes, and had a carpet bag on one side. Indianapolis was her next destination. Leaning upright against the wall beside her was the wooden trunk containing all her earthly possessions.

A piano player pounded out a raggy waltz full of rhythm and mischief. The bar brimmed with the noise of working class men in cheap black suits and stained bowlers. They told jokes and laughed raucously. The bartender juggled glasses in the air. Smoke floated in a gray-blue layer.

Emily, the older domestic from the house, entered with a businessy look and a package the size of a book, wrapped in plain white paper. Emily wore a coat over her domestic's uniform. Kate had been expecting something like this.

Spotting Kate in the corner, Emily walked toward her.

Kate pretended to ignore her. Best play it cool.

Emily said: "Claire dearie, or whatever you call yourself now that you're no longer working with us—how are you?"

"Fine, until you came in."

"I came to show you something, Claire."

"Don't scheme too much—you'll hurt your head."

"Speaking of schemes! Oh I seen how you operate. Very clever, girl. The boss ain't such a bad egg—just a bit weak for silky young skin. Likes to wander his fingers under a girl's dress for a little feel now and then."

"I wouldn't know—you tell me."

"If you say so. I got a business preppy-sition for you. Seeing as how clever you are."

Kate yawned and said: "I'm listening."

Emily put her package on the table and said: "I seen how you went after him. There's a maid here and there that will let herself be stroked for a dollar, without anything serious more. Or a look at something pink. It happens. But you, my girl, you bring it on and then whack them on the peckie. No no no! Bad boy! Pay up or else!"

"You already got a load of gin on, this time of day?"

"Deny it then. I don't care. I'm not here to make trouble. See what I got."

Kate casually hoisted her beer and eyeballed the package. With the white paper, it looked pharmaceutical. "I don't deal in stolen opiates of any kind. No cocaine, heroin, pills, or needles."

"Nothing like that, Claire. This is right up your alley. Take a look."

Unwrapping the package, Kate saw a stack of letters. "What are these?"

"Them are love notes."

Kate examined one love note, on fine paper. "They're unsigned. What good is that?"

"Does the name Spreckels mean anything to you?"

"Spreckels. The sugar people. My no-longer boss's employer."

Emily said: "That's right. I bet you never worked there. They got a huge mansion here in town, with lots of serving staff. I'm surprised you ain't gotten keen on that, but here's your chance."

Kate started reading one letter after another.

Emily said: "Twenty bucks, they're all yours."

Kate said while reading: "John Spreckels was having an affair with a young lady. He must had been quite gooey to write these."

Emily said: "Oh it was all noise. You know how men are. Promise anything for a little coussy."

Kate glowed as she held up one letter. "What do you know? Here's one from her to him. She's a domestic!"

Emily said: "Was, dearie, was. This girl, Charlotte Barnard, was a total lag, if you know what I mean. The dust was faster than her." She made slow dusting motions with a dumb face. "Mrs. Spreckels let her go. If the girl had your tits, she'd 'a gone right to the old lady with her story."

Kate kept reading. "No money in that. She'd ruin her references. Spreckels probably paid her to shut up and leave town, without his old lady getting wise."

Emily said: "Want them? Twenty bucks. I ain't offering again."

Kate said: "Where'd you get these?"

Emily said: "Charlotte. She asked me to safeguard them for her until she could burn them, but she left town and never came back."

Kate said: "You know where she went?"

Emily said: "Michigan somewheres. She won't find work in this town for a long time. You know how the grapevine goes, especially for temporary help. The slightest bad word or a dirty look, and you're finished. Like you are, here, as of now."

Kate said: "Memories are short. Takes a year or two and nobody remembers." She patted her hand on the letters. "They're nice, but they are unsigned—not even initials?"

Emily, still on the topic of blackmail, said knowingly: "Or you use a different name again."

"Don't try to be more clever than you really are, Emily."

Emily said: "The point is—it really happened. I know two girls who saw them a couple of times, slipping into his office with that look between them. Point is—he'd remember it, if you chose to bring it to his attention. You're the only one I know that has that much nerve."

Kate said: "How do I know you didn't forge the letters? I pay you, and there really was no Charlotte Barnard."

Emily said: "You can find some samples of his handwriting to compare if you want. I swear—they are the real thing."

Kate said: "Ten bucks."

Emily said: "Fifteen."

Kate said: "I'll bring the money to your apartment. Where do you live?"

Emily packed the letters away and rose. She scribbled on a card and said: "There's my address. Come up for a drink and some fun, eh?"

A swirling mist descended upon the harbor. Lights went on early, and people hurried about looking cold. Lanterns burned aboard moored ships as the fog deepened.

Kate stood in the shadows of a narrow alley, dressed in dark clothing. She kept her eye on a battered door of no particular color across the way.

As dusk fell, the first tendrils of fog crept up from the harbor.

The alley reeked of poverty. It abounded with dirty children and drunken women and sallow men whose arms bore needle tracks. This quarter was a mosaic of empty faces with idiot grins and missing teeth and vacant eyes. People moved about like shadows, like the half-dead, ghosts already.

A lamplighter came by with his wick on a stick, singing off-key. It was kind of a nice little ditty, soaked in brandy and nudged up and down the scales with schoolboy effort, but also an air of resignation amid gray beard stubble. He sang too softly to leave an echo as he passed through like a leaf falling from a tree.

A woman shouted, a door slammed, a man cursed, a dog barked, a child cried, a dove fluttered, a flying bottle shattered. And so it went.

The battered door opened and a drunken Emily staggered forth.

Kate watched as Emily lurched down the lane and into a tavern.

A ghostly shadow, Kate crossed the alley in a few blinks of the eye.

Kate groped her way up a dark, dank, smelly stairwell.

She came to a door, and rattled the knob, but it was locked.

She looked left and right.

She held her purse over her elbow, and smashed a small glass pane in the door. Reaching in, she unlocked the door and entered.

She fumbled on the walls, found a gas lamp, and lit a faint yellow light. Gas whispered and sputtered softly around her as she searched.

She tossed the place, throwing things into a pile in the middle of the room. There wasn't much to search. All of Emily's meager possessions flew onto the bare floor in minutes.

In the bedroom, Kate found the letters buried amid dirty linen in a corner on the floor. Slipping the package under her arm, she headed back down the stairs. From the doorway, she peered left and right. Then, walking calmly, she disappeared into deepening night and fog.

4. Detroit—Early Fall 1892

A doorway brooded over an iron catwalk high above the work floor of Winn & Hammond, Bookbinders. The door had a sign on it, reading *General Manager*. Coarse female laughter sickered through the twilight of grimy windows, littered work benches, and hunched women. The air smelled of paper, glue, and machine oil.

Lizzie's seat was empty. The closed door marked *Foreman* spoke volumes. May Wyllie looked embarrassed while the other women, some missing teeth, most quite rough, laughed and jeered softly. They kept their heads down and their postures workmanlike.

The door above opened. The General Manager, a stern older man in starched shirt and stiff clothes, walked out with arms akimbo. He stopped to stare at the women, who promptly fell silent and bowed deeper over their work. The General Manager walked deliberately down the steel steps, one clattering step at a time, and then on the concrete toward the Foreman's door.

A vicious crone muttered: "There you go, Sister May. The whore is about to get found out, and the hound with her." Stifled laughter erupted all around the table. May rose, threw aside her work, and tore at the other woman's hair.

The General Manager rattled John Longfield's door knob. The door was locked from within. The General Manager came prepared, however—he fished a spare key from his vest pocket, and turned it in the lock. The door swung open. There they were—lovers, half naked, frozen in shock and shame, atop Longfield's desk. They were mussy-haired and sweaty, cheeks flushed with passion and now shame, as they fumbled into their clothes.

The General Manager turned and pointed to May. His voice was harsh as whip-cracks. "For starters, you are terminated. Get out! The rest of you, back to work or I'll fire you all."

The General Manager entered John's office and slammed the door.

A short time later, a tearful May and sobbing Lizzie clung together as they hurried down a bleak street that was beginning to rustle with the first wind-blown, brown leaves of fall.

Not far away went a stooped, gloomy John Longfield shuffled off in another direction, carrying a leather satchel of tools.

❧   ❧

Lizzie and May sat with teary, smeared, swollen faces at the table. Mrs. Wyllie served them hot oatmeal and coffee.

Elizabeth said: "So that's it. This is what it's come to. I am alone, a widow, barely making ends meet, taking in sewing and cleaning as I can, working my fingers to the bone. Now where will the rent and food money come from?" She bent close to Lizzie and said: "You fool! Look what you have done to yourself and your poor sister! You must be totally daffy, to make the same mistake over and over again, without learning a lesson! Next you'll be knocked up and there we go through all that again!"

❧   ❧

Far away, in the evening at a foggy railway station in San Francisco, Kate Morgan stood in line at the ticket counter. She had just come from Emily's tenement flat, where she had taken away the Spreckels love notes. She looked over her shoulders several times. A porter wheeled her trunk to the baggage car.

Kate reached across the counter and put down a ticket and some dollar bills under the window. "I bought a ticket to Indianapolis recently. I want to exchange it."

The ticket agent said: "And where to, Miss?"

Kate said: "To Detroit." She choked excitedly. "Michigan."

❧   ❧

The transcontinental railroad was a marvel of its age, as was the telegraph. Kate Morgan, dressed nicely for travel, sat on a wooden train bench in third class. She cut an apple with a paring knife, eating slowly, bite for bite, while she once again compared one of sugar mogul John Spreckels' and domestic Charlotte Barnard's love letters with samples of Spreckels' handwriting that she had obtained.

Meanwhile, the train rumbled its stately, rhythmic *clackity-clack*.

Kate had many hours to spare before she would reach Michigan, but she'd already seen enough to convince her the letters were real. She considered the vast fortune owned by the Spreckels family, and the possibilities for the largest score she had yet made, and might ever make if she had the nerve. As she examined herself, and clutched the locket at her neck, she knew she did have the nerve. She had nothing to lose, and everything to gain.

These trains had a class system. In first class coaches, better-off families sat on upholstered, spacious seats. White-jacketed waiters served them appetizing treats. In second class coaches, passengers sat jammed together in separate compartments with upholstered seats. Kate preferred the anonymity and crowding of third class. The working poor rode on hard wooden benches.

Kate ate a sandwich from wax paper on her lap as she read. She savored pungent innuendos and verbal frolicking suggesting Mr. Spreckels'd had quite a sexual romp. How nice being able to afford such fun with a poor but beautiful girl, scrubbing her hands and knees raw at the dirt in his house. *Oh, yes, Mr. Spreckels, what if you had a little come-uppance for a change?*

Kate sipped hot coffee from a thermos as she schemed. She envisioned a Robin Hood scheme, stealing from the wealthy to enrich the poor, meaning herself. She had next to nothing, except her previous master's little blood money for her silence, so he could keep tormenting and fondling innocent young women. There had to be an angle. There always was an angle. What was the angle, the hinge, on which her strategy upon Mr. Spreckels would turn? Visiting his latest victim would help her figure that out. She hugged herself and shuddered at the thrill of coming into several thousand dollars—her largest haul to date, if she could pull it off. Surely Spreckels must value his privacy and good name that much. A plan began to take amorphous shape. Spreckels would value his good name, and she would see that he feared for it. It was just a matter of putting the right playing cards on the table for this game to begin. And it must be soon if she were to capitalize on Charlotte Barnard's folly. Passing countryside turned from Western mountains and deserts to Central plains, and eventually Eastern forests starting to turn Fall colors.

5. Knocked Up & Ruined

Not long into autumn, May Wyllie stood forebodingly before the bathroom door in her mother's house. Her face radiated worry. She knocked again, and whispered: "Lizzie?"

The door opened, revealing her sister, who stood with her hands folded before her as if in penance, shaking her head. Her eyes were full of anguish. May raised her hands to her face in horror. Her poor sister! Not again! A tear ran down each of Lizzie's cheeks—the first of many.

Arm in arm, the sisters took the first of many walks to counter the numbing shock that overtook Lizzie. Mother didn't know yet, but you couldn't hide something like this from her for long.

The streets of the city became barren as summer turned into autumn, and the two sisters went for forlorn walks, thinking of ways to find money to help their mother and keep up the household. Lizzie was much in despair over John's on again, off again attentions. Sometimes it seemed as if he were going to leave his wife and children, and at other times it seemed he was abandoning Lizzie. May could only comfort Lizzie and warn her of any further contact with their former boss.

"The game has changed now, Lizzie."

"I know, I know, I have been a fool again. But I still hope."

"You hope what?"

"That he will leave her for me. I'm younger and far prettier, for one thing. And I am willing to work."

"You're carrying his child. You won't work with a little one depending on you to be there every second."

"I couldn't bear to give it up again," Lizzie said with tears springing forth. "I would rather die."

Leaves whirled around the young women's long dresses as they walked along gray and industrial streets.

As the days grew shorter, lights stayed on in houses and lingered into the early evenings.

The very air looked gray and sad, foreboding and gloomy.

Everything had a hard, mean look, even the gleaming surfaces of a black carriage pulled by a single horse. An old man smoking a pipe sat on top, in a torn wool coat. The coach lights glimmered faintly in little brass lanterns with red glass windows as the carriage clip-clopped out of sight. It reminded Lizzie of a last, fading glimmer of hope.

Kate Morgan walked along a country lane in Michigan, having crossed the country by train. She was relieved to be away from the Transcontinental Railroads on which she and Tom had shared such mischief.

It was early fall, and there was still a little green in the trees, but the light was sad and beautiful, and many of the leaves had dried into the colors of apples—bright yellows and somber reds and purples.

She arrived at a brick mansion with ivied walls and a magnificent front.

Walking around the back, she came to a servants' entrance and knocked. A pretty young woman in maid's uniform came to the door. "Yes?"

Kate said: "I'm looking for Charlotte Barnard."

Charlotte Barnard said: "That's me."

Kate said: "My name is Lucy Crawford. I just came from San Francisco."

Charlotte Barnard looked horrified. "Is it something I done?"

Kate said: "No, no, I came to give you this." She handed over a love note. "Emily says she waited a time, then burned them all—but she forgot that one."

Charlotte snatched the love note and stared at it open-mouthed. "Oh my God. I thought I was done with this. Now I'll burn this one and it's all behind me."

Kate said: "Charlotte, I can't stay long because I am taking a position in Detroit, and have to show up there tomorrow. Apparently, Mr. Spreckels got in hot water with his old lady over a little fling with you."

Charlotte Barnard cried: "My new employer must hear nothing about it. Nothing! Or I'm ruined!"

Kate said: "Hush, dear. There won't be a word. Does Spreckels know where to find you?"

"Oh God, I hope not."

Kate said: "Wonderful. I'm a bit curious. Such a wealthy man. What was he like?"

Charlotte looked furtively around. She seemed nervous, but eager to learn what she could from Kate, just as Kate was eager to learn from her about Spreckels. "Why do you want to know?"

Kate said: "Just nosey as the dickens."

Charlotte Barnard grinned: "I have a little time. Would you like to come in for tea?"

"I've been walking for a few hours, and I could use something hot."

Charlotte Barnard said: "We have hot soup in the kitchen. And bread. Come on in, and I'll give you a mouthful and an earful. All the gossip. They are an interesting family. Now about John Spreckels..."

❧   ☙

In Detroit, streets were piled deeply with golden and dark apple-red leaves. Trees looked twisted and barren. Days were short—gray and rainy, except for a few stand-out sunny days.

Mrs. Elizabeth Wyllie had found out about Lizzie's new out-of-wedlock pregnancy. An argument was on in the apartment, where light seeped wanly through the kitchen window. Mrs. Wyllie walked up and down yelling amid her few pieces of shabby furniture May tried to step between her mother and sister. Lizzie sniffled into one of several hankies with the monogram *Lizzie Anderson*. They were her mother's. Elizabeth said: "I can't stand it any more. You got yourself knocked up again, Lizzie. How could you be so stupid?"

May said: "Easy, Mom. She's fragile."

Elizabeth said: "Fragile! Am I a brown bear? She wasn't fragile to be carrying on with that wolf in his lair!"

Lizzie said: "I can't stand it any longer! He loves me; I love him."

Elizabeth said: "If that man loves you, Lizzie, then I am a Christmas tree. Are you daffy? He's a married man with children, out of work, and broke. What can he possibly do for you? He has ruined you, all for his craven lust and selfishness."

Lizzie held her fists over her ears. "I can't think! I can't think! You drive me crazy!"

"I drive you crazy?" Her mother sniffed. "Hah. I'll soon be committed."

May said: "Have you heard from him lately?"

Lizzie sniffled, wiping a wrist across her face. "Not a peep so far this week."

May said: "He's dumped you, girl. Showed you the street. We'll see about that."

⤳ ⤵

L eaves swirled thickly in damp, chill air the color of smoke, and people wore thick clothing. In an arched brick portal, framed in ivy, May stood before a chastened John Longfield. "I'll not let you just throw her away, Mr. Longfield."

John said: "I care greatly about your sister. I'll do what a man must do."

May said: "Oh, and what's that, Mr. Longfield? Leave your wife and children? And you have no job, no money to feed them?"

John said: "May, please, it's already all so difficult."

May said: "It'll be far worse if I go to your wife and pour out the truth. Your poor wife, Mr. Longfield. Think about her and your children."

John cringed. "You wouldn't do that to me."

May said: "See, it's always about you. You could implore me not to do that to her. Lizzie is knocked up, Mr. Longfield, by you."

"I know. She's told me. You've told me."

"So what are you going to do?"

"That's the question, isn't it? What would you do, May?"

"I have no idea. I didn't get myself into such a mess."

"I'm puzzling over it, trust me, until my brain hurts."

May said: "You created this puzzle for yourself."

John said: "Lizzie created hers too. She got herself into it."

May said: "Don't give me that, you son of a bitch. You ruined my sister. You can walk away, a bounder, a hound, but my poor sweet sister—who is naive and innocent and lacks common sense, as much as she is elegant and beautiful and has a head full of airy dreams about being an actress, when she can't remember a cake recipe, much less lines on stage— you used this poor dear girl like a common whore and now you don't know what to do. Well, Mr. Longfield, short of tossing yourself under a train, you'd better come up with something good. And soon."

May turned and strode away, leaving a troubled John Longfield to consider his options.

Lizzie sat in third class on a train chuffing through early autumn Michigan countryside. Its severe beauty was enough to make you cry. It was like reading one of those fallen angel books. She looked anxiously about, and occasionally pulled out a hankie to sniffle into it. Eventually, she passed a sign that read: *Grand Rapids 5 Mi*. From the train station it was a blurry, tearful trip to Aunt Louisa's house. She rode on a wagon pulled by a horse, driven by an older man wearing a red cap. The wagon was from the train station, and held her three trunks. Lizzie rode up to a private residence in a working class but clean neighborhood. She ran up the steps and knocked on the door, while the porter brought her trunks to the porch, one by one. Lizzie tipped him and he departed, touching his cap.

The door opened and a woman resembling Lizzie's mother opened. Louisa Anderson brightened and opened her arms lovingly. "Lizzie, my sweet, favorite niece. Oh how good to see you, baby."

They embraced, and Lizzie started crying again

"Come on in, sweetheart," said Aunt Louisa. She put her arm around Lizzie and guided her into the dark, spacious comfort of her house. As she did so, Louisa, a spinster, called for a male friend who was doing work in the house to fetch Lizzie's three trunks.

Louisa sat on the couch while Lizzie sat opposite her. Louisa's male friend, having taken the trunks upstairs to a spare bedroom, stirred his coffee. He was a powerful but gentle looking man in his forties, in a worn herringbone suit, white shirt, and burgundy silk necktie worn shiny.

Lizzie sobbed wetly into a hankie embroidered *Lizzie Anderson*.

The man said: "Poor girl—she's beside herself."

Aunt Louisa said: "Lizzie darling, is that your last hankie? Your mother's old hankies yet—she does love you, even if she throws you out—but sends you away with her personal hankies."

"Well, it's not like she threw me out—I actually left on my own."

"Oh, I know, darling, but she does have a temper. She must have been impossible. I'm sure I know what it's all about, and we'll talk about it when you catch a hold of yourself." She extended a hand for the hankie, which looked soppy and ready to be washed. "Here," Louisa said. "I'll give you some of mine."

Louisa went to a cupboard and took out a half dozen embroidered hankies, which she put on the table near Lizzie. She took the wet one away to wash. The fresh hankies were stitched *Louisa Anderson*. Her mother and aunt had received a combined gift set as little girls.

Aunt Louisa returned from the laundry chute in the kitchen. "You're welcome to stay here as long as you like. So your mother is upset with you? Oh, you'll tell me, won't you? And you came for refuge in my house. When you're able to speak, you can pour out the whole sad drama to me. Whatever it is, I won't think any the less of you. My sister will get over her fuss, and your dear sweet sister May is such a steady mate that you'll always have her support."

6. Detroit—Kate, Lizzie, & John

Kate Morgan stepped from the servants' entrance of a splendid mansion in a better neighborhood of Detroit. The day was done. She was among several other female domestics who bid each other good night.

Kate wore a coat over her domestic's garb, and strode briskly down a tree-lined, cobblestone street that was damp from rain and littered with bright yellow and dull russet leaves. After a few blocks, on a main cross street, she boarded an electric trolley.

She sat among a crowd of people employed much like she was. She felt anonymous, though she still looked around fearfully from time to time. As she and her fellow passengers rocked about, she thought about her grand scheme.

How could she pull off a job on Spreckels? It must be carefully planned, effective, and safe. No doubt, the more important the man, the more he would worry for his reputation. Suppose a big man like that got a girl in trouble. Wouldn't other companies cancel their orders from him? What would his wife think? What if he had daughters? It must be humiliating.

She felt a bit like Archimedes, who'd said something like "Give me a big enough lever, and I can move the world." The love notes were her lever, but were they lever enough?

The trolley hummed on its tracks along pleasantly littered streets, among the cozy-lit windows of good homes, and into a shabbier part of Detroit. There, she got off and walked deeper and deeper into the heart of the working people's quarter. On the way to her rented room in a boarding house for women domestics of virtue, she spotted a random tavern and decided her tired whistle could use a cool, tasty, sudsy beer.

  ❦ ❧

May Wyllie and John Longfield stood huddled in the same covered archway where she had confronted him a day earlier. She had summoned him again. John said: "How is she, May?"

May said: "She's with our Aunt Louisa in Grand Rapids. My poor mother gets crazier by the day."

John said: "I'm a stupid bastard. If you want me to throw myself off a bridge, I'll gladly do it if it will help."

"We need to have it taken care of. She can't go through all that again."

John said: "I have no money or means to help, May—I'm sorry. I cherish your sister very much. I'll do anything I can."

May said: "Can I trust you then, Mr. Longfield? Will you do one thing right for us all?"

John said: "On my heart, I swear it. On my dead mother's grave."

May said: "I know a woman in Cleveland, who is very good at helping girls in trouble. She's a school-taught nurse, clean, and knows what she is doing. She'll finish in less than hour if all goes well. Lizzie needs a man with her on the trip. Can you take her there and watch out for her?"

"On my soul, May. Have you got the money for it? I sure don't."

May reluctantly held up a wad of money in a gilded clip. "My savings. I took up a collection from my girl friends. Promise me you will use it to help my sister." She handed it over. "Lizzie was nearly destroyed last time, having the baby and then giving it up because that's what they made her do. She couldn't go through that again, and she is nowhere near ready to have a child, especially unmarried, no money, and on her own. It's our only chance to save her life and her reputation."

John took the money clip. "On my life, May. I'll be on the train to Grand Rapids first thing to get Lizzie. I pray all goes well. I'll leave the poor angel alone."

"If you screw up, Mr. Longfield, you'll have me to deal with."

"I know it, May. I promise I'll be good."

In a Detroit tavern, men and women sang rowdy songs amid beer and good cheer as Kate walked to a side counter of the bar. Waiting her turn, she ordered food and drink. She looked around at the pool players and card players and dark players. She bought a beer, and a German sausage on a roll with spicy mustard. Then she found herself a little table in a corner and dug in with hunger and thirst.

She began to notice a man playing cards at a nearby table. He kept peeling bills off of a gilded clip, and he was losing. Kate watched in detached amusement as the man looked increasingly desperate. He was a handsome, if disreputable looking fellow, with a nice face, a pencil mustache, and heavy beard shadow. He had seductive, boyish, dark blue eyes and strong but soft white hands. Kate looked his lean, well-proportioned body up and down in his wool, herringbone suit. He lost—again and again. And he'd had a few beers too many, but he was holding his liquor well. She liked that in a man. He didn't seem like the violent type, and he looked like he needed a hand.

Kate finished her sandwich and washed it down with a rich, heady mug of beer with a thick mustache of white foam on it. She felt tired from her day's work, but eating and drinking and being around people made her feel better again. She liked being among people, though she did not form relationships with them, unless it was through the filter of her disguises and ruses, by which she could control the situation. This man interested her, and she daydreamed about having him in bed with her.

The man angrily rose and tossed his cards aside. Unlike Tom, this one looked sort of helpless and harmless in his anger. He stomped to the bar. He ordered a beer and stood darkly sucking on it, wrapping himself around it as if nursing his wounded feelings. Several times, he glanced resentfully at the red-haired man who had cleaned him out. Red was already taking yet another man's money while grinning smugly and taunting him softly. Kate felt her pulse quicken as she read her blue-eyed man's mind. She watched as Blue-Eyes sneaked out the back door. She quickly grew more and more interested. From the trapped look in his eyes, she had an idea what the beaten young man was planning.

Shortly, Red rose and picked up his coat. He bid his fellow card players good night and headed for the door. Kate thought he looked smug and mean-eyed as he shoved the door open on his way out. Kate rose with her beer and sidled over to the window. Pulling the curtain slightly aside, she peered out. Red walked past the window toward the trolley station, whistling, with his head held high. Blue-Eyes moved stealthily after him.

Kate drained her beer, wiped her wrist across her mouth, grabbed her purse, and sidled out the door.

Red walked happily toward the lights of a distant street and trolley stop. His path ran along a sidewalk that made a wide curve around a dark church yard full of shadowy bushes.

Kate moved after him like a shadow among shadows. In a few seconds, she spotted her man hunkering under the shadows of the purplish blocks of the church wall. It was clear he planned to jump the red-haired man in a few seconds as he rounded the curve, but he looked desperate and unsure of himself. This was no fearless Tom Morgan with guns, and he endeared himself to her instantly. Blue-Eyes hunkered under a large tree, veiled in darkness. Blue-Eyes looked at her as if caught with his pants down. She almost laughed at his bunny-like face of pale terror. He'd already missed his chance. Red was several seconds past on his way to the trolley station.

Kate walked up to blue-eyes, staying on the sidewalk. "I saw you lose your money. I know what you're about to do."

He said: "Lady, I need that money back. It's life or death."

"Let me help you out." She hailed the red haired man: "Sir!" Kate's new companion ducked back down.

Red turned. "Yes?" His face flickered through a range of expressions and possibilities.

Kate said: "I think you lost something here in the bushes."

Red licked his lips with nervous hunger. "I did, did I?"

Kate said: "Something mighty nice, for a very small price."

Red said: "I'll have to come look at it then."

Kate said: "You'll be a happy man, and I'll be a happy gal—we could even split a beer afterward."

Red came back down the sidewalk. "A sweet way to end a lovely night!" Face radiant with expectation, he put his arm around Kate's waist. She touched the hardness in his pants, and he moaned. Together, they stepped into the bushes and darkness under the great tree. She heard the ragged sawing of his excited breath. He moaned with anticipation. He leaned eagerly down to put his lips on Kate's mouth. Just the right moment, she thought as she cold-cocked him with a hard fist. He staggered backward with fluttering eyes.

Blue-Eyes rose up from behind and hit him with a brick, dropping him cold. He pulled Red's body deeper into the bushes.

Kate said: "Don't kill him. Just grab the money. He'll stay put a while." From her copious experience with men, Red would not report that he was mugged by a prostitute in the bushes outside a church. His shame would overcome his moral outrage. Pecker pride was a man's Achilles Heel.

Her new partner in crime emerged, counting his wad of money.

Kate stretched forth her palm and said: "My share."

He stared at her, open-mouthed.

Kate said: "Don't even think of stiffing me. I helped you get your money back, that you lost in there. I want my cut. Or I'll start screaming bloody murder. And if the guy's dead..."

He said: "Aw hell, he's alive. Just out cold. Here, thank you, I wasn't thinking—I'll give you five. How's that?"

Kate said: "Ten, or I start piping like a steam ship."

He meekly handed over the money.

"What's your name?"

"John Longfield. What's yours?"

"Kate Morgan." As they conversed, they walked into the street. Soon she felt comfortable with this John Longfield. She put her arm around his arm. "I have a feeling we'll do well together, don't you? I'm thirsty. How about sharing a beer?"

"Sounds good to me." He winked. "I'll buy. I made a few bucks on this deal. He cleaned a few others out." John put his arm around her waist. "You won't sock me, will you?"

It dawned on her—she'd made a mistake, and used her real name. *Oh well*, she thought, *I'll bed this stray cat one night, we'll have our fun, and I'll never see him again*. She laughed. "Only if you deserve it." She welcomed the sensuous touch of his hand, which timidly probed the curve of her waist, feeling the sturdiness of her torso. His fingertips probed as far as he dared down the softness of her belly. Then he ran his palm over the generous curve of her thigh and buttock. She pushed his hand away, but kept an arm around his waist. He felt hard and muscular. Her one hand lingered on the ridge of his hip, and with her other fingers brushed over the rocky flatness of his rippling abdomen. Kate said: "Let's find a cozy little crib, and you can tell me all about yourself."

A few hours later, John Longfield and Kate Morgan were in bed in a shabby hotel. John had paid for their beers, as promised, and he'd paid for the night here. Kate felt a languid sense of generosity and wanted to repay him with something sweet. She did not want him to know about her room not far away, nor could she bring him there. Here, where nobody asked questions, a blanket covered them on a fresh but rude bed. The sheets were clean, but stiff. Their smell had an alkaline bite of cheap soap. John and Kate were naked. Their clothes hung thrown over a chair. Their bare shoulders and faces were sweaty from sex. He noticed she wore a gold locket on a chain around her neck. He was still on top, as they exchanged languid kisses. She was a lively mare of a woman. "You wear me out, my sweet." He palmed her thigh. "And I love it." He rolled over beside her.

Kate loved his boyish, irresponsible grin. "My handsome playboy." She planted a string of kisses across his features. "I'm tired, honey, and I have to be at work early." She'd had experience with boys very early, even before Tom, but had never cheated on him, not even in their last few years together, when he'd been terrible to her. Since she'd left him, she'd had an occasional quick fling. Tom had been the love of her life, and she never expected to trust a man again or get involved, and had no intention of it with this one, but she knew she would be a little taken with this one and maybe let him under her skin a bit, as long as he didn't hit her or drink too much. Men were men—there was no changing them. Evolution had worked for women, but men had remained monkeys. She took his sex in her hand and played with it tenderly.

John said: "Where do you work?"

Kate said: "I am a substitute maid. I work all over. A day here, a week there. If a maid has to visit her dying mother, or a maid is out sick, they hire me for the short term." She felt him grow hard in her hand again. Did this boy have a full coal tender, always ready to roll and toot? What surprised her was that she didn't want him to conquer her. She wanted to take him, safely control him, enjoy him at arms' length. She sighed deeply, shuddering, realizing how much she needed a man, and here he was.

John pressed himself upon her once more. She put him into her, and they rocked together with eyes closed. John said: "I want you, oh God I want you."

Kate said: "I want you too, sweetheart. I've been pretty lonely, working for those stiff-neck phonies up in the good part of town." She chortled softly. "They have no idea about the good parts of town." She reached down under the covers and palmed his behind. "But I do."

John groaned and gasped as she expertly rocked him to climax. They moaned together, holding each other. His climax excited her over the top.

He whispered: "Where did you learn these tricks? Where do you come from, woman? Where do they make women like you?"

"You really want to know?"

John nodded as they lay quietly, side by side, in the soft light..

Kate said: "I was born in Hamburg, Iowa, named Katie Farmer. My mother died when I was young. I grew up restless, before the trains came through. I was a wild kid, the devil to my poor widowed dad and my grandfather. I am from a wealthy miller's family."

John said: "With all that money, why did you leave them?"

Kate said: "I never could sit still or behave. On a freezing cold day, one of the worst winters in many years, I married a young fellow named Thomas Morgan. He had the same wild streak I did, and we understood each other well, soul to soul. My grandfather, Joe Chandler—he knew I was hard of heart and harder of head. The Transcontinental Railroad came in, which was good for the millers to send their flour far and wide, but Tom and I, we caught the travel bug and ran off to see the world. Once we saw those wonderful trains going far and wide, we couldn't stop ourselves. We did some nasty tricks on people to stay flush." She giggled.

"And this man of yours?"

"He turned mean, beat me bloody, threw me down the stairs. I can never have children again. So I left him, and I haven't seen him in several years. I hope I never lay eyes on him again."

"Ah. So you have no children then." It was as much a question as a polite comment. Kate was silent for a while. He stroked her face with his fingers, kissed her gently, and enjoyed being with her. That softened her up, and she cuddled close to him. She touched her locket and said tenderly, breaking up in tears a bit: "Tom and I had a fine little boy. My little Eddie. He lived just two days, the poor little angel. I don't know why he was taken. He lived long enough to have a little name all his own—Eddie. That's all he got—two nights and one day of grim, icy gray winter, and then he was taken. Tom and I went a long time before I became pregnant again, and then he got drunk and threw me down the stairs. I can't have children now. After that I left him. And I still look over my shoulder every day. I'm afraid of him." She started crying.

John comforted her with kisses and tender words. She held onto him tightly. "You be good to me."

"I will," John promised. He felt himself growing hard again.

Kate said: "I've been on my own ever since. I've figured out how to take care of myself. That's all it is. Taking care of yourself in a world that takes your babies. There's a rich family named Spreckels in San Francisco where I worked. They had thirteen children. Only five lived. They lost eight—so what kind of world is this?"

John said: "I know, I know. A tough one. And you have to know how to get through the day and not let the other dogs run off with your bone. You figure losing Eddie made you tough?"

Kate said: "Oh no, the other way around. I was plenty tough. That made me understand what it was to feel something. It softened me a bit. I thank Eddie for it every day. I always had a hard time feeling for other people. Now I cry when I think of that." She sniffled.

A while later, Kate and John lay drowsily in each other's arms. They nuzzled slowly on their way to sleep.

John said: "Wake me when you get up."

"Are you going to work too?"

"Lost my job. I'm fixing a problem for a friend."

"And what's that, sweetie?"

"This friend of mine knocked a lady up, and I'm taking her to a doctor to get her problem fixed."

"She is pregnant?"

"Yeah. In a manner of speaking."

"How far along?" She knew, from the sound of his voice, what it was about, and she thought of her Spreckels plan.

"Can't be more than two months. Three at most."

"Level with me, Lothario. She's your piece, right?"

"Was. I wish I could shake her. I promised her sister I would take her to this woman for an abortion, but then I lost the money—I was just trying to multiply it, so to speak, so I could double it, take care of Lizzie, and still have a pile. But I ran out of luck, until you helped me, bless your soul."

"Maybe we can help each other out. By the pale of your finger, I see you're hiding a wedding ring."

"You're sharp. Actually, since I lost my job, I pawned it, along with Lizzie's earrings. My old lady's no sweat."

"I know what you mean. There's my old man dangling around someplace. So Lizzie is the name of your problem, is it?"

"One of them."

"Oh yes, the wife and kids. Well, honey, you can warm my bed for however long I am in town. I'll be no trouble to you. I'm barren as an Iowa field in winter, I don't carry disease, and I am hot as fire."

John mounted her again and said: "Oh God bless you. I do love you so. Give me some more of that. I can't stay away."

"Have all you want. There's plenty more for you—all you need." As they headed to climax, Kate held him and thrust back with all her bodily might while she goaded him: "Come on, give it to me. Give me all you've got. More! Harder! Show me you're a man. Rip me now, in me hard. No shame. Just do me down and dirty so I feel you deep…"

        ❧   ❦

Next morning, in a gray dawn light, Kate dressed. She looked tired but happy. She had her hair up in both hands, and hairpins in her mouth. "John!"

John stirred and moaned faintly. Then he sat up, rubbing his eyes. "My God, is it morning already? You wore me out last night."

"I'll wear you out plenty more, don't worry. Go get the girl, bring her to town. Get her a fancy place that she'll like."

John said: "Lizzie is so particular! She's neat and dainty like a great lady, even though she's just a fired little factory girl."

Kate threw down a few bills. "Here—get a dollar-a-day place

downtown. That should impress her. I'll tell you more this evening. I have something in store for that girl—for us three, actually."

ও⚬ ⚬৬

John Longfield took the train to get Lizzie Wyllie at her aunt's house in Grand Rapids. Aunt Louisa sent them off with mixed feelings, confused about whether this oddly good-looking yet somehow devious looking man had come to fetch her for a wedding, or something else. Seeing Lizzie's radiant face, she grew baffled and tentative, and resolved to talk more with her sister, now that Elizabeth might have calmed down a bit. She would send a telegram to Elizabeth and May.

Lizzie and John rode to the train station in the same wagon with the same three trunks. The same red-cap was driving the same horse that had brought Lizzie here just a few days earlier. Lizzie put her arm through John's arm, and snuggled close.

He patted her hand. "I came back to get you. Told you I would, didn't I?"

Lizzie said: "I never lost faith in you."

John said: "Your sister May and I had a talk, Lizzie. She wants me to help get you fixed up. And then we'll figure what to do next."

Lizzie'd had time to think. "I can't go through the whole thing of having the baby and giving it up again. I would rather have our child and raise it by myself, if I have to, if you'll just provide for us and come see me once or twice a week."

"I would gladly see you every day, Lizzie, but I have no job right now and I'm having trouble making ends meet."

Lizzie said slowly: "Then you want me to get rid of it."

"Well, we can think about what to do. There is a kind woman I spoke with, Kate Morgan, who wants to help us. I'm in this with you, Lizzie."

"Oh, thank you!" She gripped his arm. "Sometimes I just want you for myself. Then I realize—what am I doing? What am I thinking? It would be so unfair to you, and your wife, and your children. Then I think—you could just keep me on the side. I'd be no trouble. I could find work again, and keep a small place, and we'd have a little love nest. You'd like that, wouldn't you?"

John said: "You are the sweetest little birdie I did ever hear sing."

He knew he had no tact or feeling for these things, but his wooden comments had all the same effect on her as eloquent speech.

Lizzie said: "Hold me tight to you."

John put his arm around her and held her close.

She laughed and cried at the same time. "I'm sorry. I have all these crazy ups and downs in my condition. I'll do whatever you want me to." She took off her earrings. "Remember these? I'm going to give them back to you, in case you need money."

He examined the tiny holes in her earlobes. "Do they hurt?"

She shook her head. "Not at all. I'll have to get them re-pierced if I don't find some posts to put in soon."

He reddened. "Darling, why don't you keep them? You look so beautiful in them." He looked genuinely upset.

She laughed and hugged him. "It's just stuff. We can always get more stuff. As long as we are together, you are all the stuff that I need."

❧   ❧

Once John and Lizzie were back in Detroit, he took her to a fine hotel he had chosen. He ushered Lizzie into a sparkling hotel room with clean sheets and curtains. A bellhop followed, wheeling her three trunks. The man thoughtfully lined them up along one wall in a corner, for convenient access. John tipped the man and thanked him as he left.

Alone with John, Lizzie hugged herself and looked around. She twirled around the room, glancing at all the little touches. "This is nice."

John said: "Something special for you. For a special gal."

Lizzie sat down on the bed and patted the bed by her thigh. John sat down beside her. "I missed you so," Lizzie said as she reached for him. They struggled from their clothes, kissing ardently. She pulled the covers apart, and John kissed Lizzie as she pulled him down on her. "I've been so lonely without you."

John said: "I've been lonely without you too. You're so nice to be with."

Lizzie said: "I want you so...come here...love me!" She pulled him toward her, and his ardor grew instantly. She was far more cultured and elegant than Kate, even if she was a poor factory girl. John knew he was a rough cut who belonged with the likes of Kate. But this beautiful young woman wanted him and who was he to deny her? Especially, with this commanding and self-assured Kate Morgan in charge. Kate could do all the thinking now, and that was okay with John.

౨ ఆ

That evening, John and Kate sat in a corner by a brick wall. The large noisy tavern had many people talking and shouting. "Can you talk her into it?" Kate asked.

"I think she'll go along. She doesn't have much choice. I don't want to hurt her, Kate."

"I don't either. You'll have to trust me. We'll all be a lot richer, including her. Just a few days of discomfort, and she'll be rid of her problem, you'll be rid of yours, and everyone will live happily ever after."

"Is this going to be dangerous, Kate?"

"Don't worry. You let me handle things."

"You swear?"

She held two fingers over her heart and put on her most radiant, convincing face. "Honest Injun."

A little bit reluctantly, he set aside any nagging little doubts he still had. "Okay then—I trust you."

She gripped his wrist on the table, and leaned close with that piercing, forceful, irresistibly hypnotic gaze. "You can't just trust me, John. You have to be with me totally, a hundred percent, or this won't work."

He swallowed hard, trying to think it all through, though everything just stayed a big muddle in his mind. "I do," he said, reassured by her firm stare and her iron grip. She was stronger than any woman he'd ever met.

Kate released his arm and picked up her beer. "We'll get her out of town, where nobody will recognize her."

"You're the brain of the outfit, boss."

"Where have you stuck her?"

"First class hotel, in a nice sunny room—like you said. So what's next?"

Kate said: "We'll head for Los Angeles, with a stop in Iowa to deposit a little money. I'll fill you in on the plan as we go along. We'll kill two birds with one stone. We'll fix Lizzie right up so her baby problem goes away. Your baby problem goes away. Same time, we'll make a pile of dough."

John said: "Honestly, I'd like Lizzie to go away too. I have enough trouble on my hands, trying to feed my wife and kids. She's nice, but I'm tired of her. I'm just crazy about you."

"Don't think about leaving your family for me. I wouldn't let you."

"Maybe I can change your mind, woman."

Kate shook her head. "You'll have a snoot full of me soon enough. I can be hard on a man."

"I've never met a woman like you." He added reluctantly: "I know you know what's best. You do mean the best for me, for us, even for Lizzie."

"Sure." Kate nodded. "There's this wealthy man in San Francisco named John Spreckels. He has been buying up everything in San Diego since the financial boom there collapsed in 1889. He owns a splendid resort hotel in Coronado. I have some love letters Mr. Spreckels foolishly gave to a maid he was sweet on. I want Lizzie to play the maid. We'll tell Spreckels he got her pregnant, and order him to pay up, or else. It's really simple."

John said: "Lizzie couldn't play a maid. She can hardly play herself. Her head is full of theater posters, fancy clothes, all what she can't afford."

Kate said: "I'll train her to impersonate. I can start her in Los Angeles. I'll show her the ropes."

"So it's pay-up-or-else for this Spreckels goon? Sounds like blackmail."

Kate said: "If Mr. Spreckels doesn't wire a large amount of money to a distant bank, where we can grab it and run, then Lizzie will have her miscarriage right in his hotel lobby. You want to call that blackmail—I call it goose mail—goosing him to behave like a man."

John said: "Well, I'm sure you know best, Kate, being so sure about this and all. Sounds like he should gladly pay to avoid the embarrassment."

Kate said: "The best part is—he's too far away to investigate. There won't be time. He'll be quick to pay us off in exchange for a signed release from Charlotte Barnard."

"How you going to do that?" He stared at her owlishly.

She stared back. "I already wrote the letter." She burst out laughing. He blinked, realizing he was always slow keeping up with Kate, and then he too laughed. They were both at it, with shaking shoulders, staring at each other and giggling. When he calmed down, John asked: "What kind of sum are you talking?"

Kate said: "A lot—enough for each of us to live well for years. When you get tired of me, you can go back to your wife and kids."

John pulled at her dress and said: "You won't tire me out. "

Kate pushed his hand away: "Not now. Not here. Go take care of Lizzie. She needs you. She must never guess about you and me. We'll get Lizzie fixed and send her home with her cut. Then you and I can play all we want. But never, ever sit next to me in public or in her sight. Never touch me. Never give me that look. Save it for Lizzie." She patted his hand. "It'll be over soon, and Lizzie will be a busy girl."

7. Los Angeles—Mid-Autumn 1892

John and Lizzie sat side by side in second class on a drizzly October day. Kate sat opposite them, dark and cold, her gaze out the window.

Beautiful wide-open American countryside rolled endlessly by outside. Rain and mud slowly gave way to the wide open skies and rolling prairies of the Midwest. Lizzie clung to John like a school girl.

Kate kept driving her plan home, one small piece at a time that Lizzie could digest: "Lizzie, this man Spreckels is a very bad man. He mashed a girl named Charlotte Barnard, and ruined her career in San Francisco."

Lizzie said: "Yes?" She had her hands folded between her knees.

Kate said: "You're not going to think about him. He'll get what he deserves. He has millions of dollars, and won't miss a few thousand."

Lizzie said: "That much!"

Kate said: "I have a great plan, but you won't really need to do anything much. I'll show you how to behave. You just pretend to be Charlotte Barnard—or actually, Lottie Bernard. Mr. Spreckels will be hundreds of miles away in San Francisco. You'll be down in San Diego. You'll never see him. He'll quickly decide the best thing is to pay up and we'll leave town within a day or two. I've seen it work before."

Lizzie said: "You've done this before?"

Kate caught herself, and said with a veiled look: "I knew someone who was good at it, and I learned a few tricks from her."

Lizzie said: "And you'll teach me? I'm bright enough—just a little slow at learning. I make up for it in looks and style." John rolled his eyes, laughing kindly.

Kate said: "I'll teach you how to impersonate a maid. That's simple, right? All you do is keep your beautiful face shut, and dust. Got that?"

Lizzie made dusting motions. "Just keep dusting, huh? I think I can do that." She giggled.

Kate said: "You speak only when spoken to, and say as little as possible. Avoid small talk with the other girls. Keep to yourself. It will all be over in a few weeks, and then you'll have a lot of money."

Lizzie said: "I'll try my very best."

Kate took Lizzie's hands in both of her hands and said: "No, Lizzie, 'try' is not good enough. You have to be determined that it's going to work. It's like I told John—you have to be a hundred percent or it won't work right."

Lizzie said: "I promise. I'll give it a hundred percent." She held one of Kate's hands, and one of John's in her other hand. She looked radiantly happy in that union of love and friendship. Her lover and her friend both let her be like that for a happy minute or two. Then Kate got back to business. Kate said: "I made up a name for you. I'm going to call you Katie Logan. Can you remember that?"

Lizzie said: "Sure, that's easy."

Kate said: "I like your confidence. Now start thinking that you're Katie Logan in your head. Get used to the name. I made it easy for you to remember. I used my first name, Kate, and a family name that's close to mine, Logan instead of Morgan."

❦ ❧

John, Kate, and Lizzie arrived on the West Coast on a sunny, balmy day in early November 1892. As they walked through the Los Angeles train station, Kate said: "Lizzie, I'm sending your trunks on to San Diego. Here are the three baggage claim checks." She offered three pieces of paper, but Lizzie said: "I'm afraid I might lose them."

Kate said: "Here, John, you hold them for her."

John said: "Sure—for my sweetheart, anything." He put the tickets in his wallet. He took out the silver earrings. "See? I still have them. Holding them for my sweetheart, and I swear I always will."

Lizzie tugged bravely at her earlobes, which were closing up.

Kate said: "Lizzie, you sure you won't lose your nerve? You can't come running to me or John. You have to stay on the job and not get fired."

Lizzie said: "I've been a hard-working girl for years. I know how to keep my nose to the grindstone. "

Kate said: "Great. Well, then, let's go find a hotel. You two lovers should spend at least one night together before our adventure starts. I'll see you in the morning, Lizzie."

❧ ❧

In a darkened hotel room, John and Lizzie made love, and then lay together in sweaty lethargy. John said: "That Kate is a thinker, huh?"

Lizzie said: "She'll save me from ruination. You and I will have a lot of money to make a new life together." She touched his nose, trying to push home her point. He always became evasive about staying with her. It made her uneasy deep down, but she always pushed the thought away. If he did not love her, then she was ruined for sure. It was to scary to be possible.

He sensed her feelings and said: "Don't worry so much. Don't think too far ahead. Just think about how you're going to manage this impersonation thing in the next couple of weeks."

Lizzie sighed and lay back in a blind rush of desperation and hope. She had no choice but to trust John and this kind stranger, Kate Morgan.

John put his arm around her. Comforted, she said: "Katie Logan, Katie Logan, Katie Logan..." She laughed. "See? I have it down pat."

John mumbled a reassurance, gave her a gentle shake, and started snoring. She turned over and spooned her back against his front. His warmth made her drowsy and pushed her worries away as she drifted off.

❧ ❧

In the early morning, Lizzie and Kate stood near a wealthy home. Kate handed Lizzie an envelope. "Here is a letter of recommendation I got my Uncle Will Farmer to write for me. He's an important grower in Hanford and Visalia. I've changed the name on the letter to Katie Logan for you." She added: "Your employer is Mrs. R. M Widney. I'll send my own trunk along for storage. Pretend it's yours, since your three trunks will be at the baggage depot in San Diego."

Lizzie said: "I promise I will do very well. I like how you've planned everything out to the last detail."

Kate said: "Where are your glasses?"

Lizzie stared at her—then, reluctantly, produced a pair of wire-rimmed glasses from her purse.

Kate said: "Be sure you have them so you're not blind as a bat and mix things up." She fluffed Lizzie's clothing. "Make sure you look presentable. But then you're a clothes horse. Be brave. Just keep your mouth shut and keep dusting. They don't expect conversation or entertainment from you. For all they care, a domestic is just another piece of furniture. In some homes, husband and wife have their most private arguments right in front of you, as if you were an ottoman or a sofa."

Lizzie laughed and said: "This will be an adventure."

Kate said: "You'll get used to being someone other than you, and in a few weeks you'll be ready for your dramatic stage entrance in Coronado."

Lizzie said: "I love acting and actresses."

Kate said: "I know you do. But honey, for God's sake, these will be roles without speaking parts." She gave Lizzie a brief hug. "Good luck!" With that, she walked away.

L izzie took a deep breath and then walked up to the main door. She knocked, and a voice called for her to enter. For a moment, she felt apprehensive. A kind lady sat at a desk in the parlor as Lizzie entered. Mrs. Widney said: "Hello, dear. You must be Katie Logan."

Lizzie looked stunned for an instant, then caught herself and said: "Yes." She was in for it now. She was in the swim, and there was no turning back. She felt strangely calm, knowing that Kate Morgan had thought everything through.

The lady rose, smiling graciously, and pointed to a hallway. Mrs. Widney said: "My regular upstairs girl is on vacation. You seem entirely acceptable, my dear. Your reference letters from Mr. Farmer is very strong. Our interview need not continue. Go down that hallway and introduce yourself to the Head of Staff."

Lizzie spent a week with the Widneys, and became totally immersed in her work and in the strange sensation of being someone other than herself. Kate was right. It was fun, it was exciting, it was interesting—and easy. She felt as if she finally had an opportunity at acting, and found she was very good at it.

❧ ❧

As during last week with the Widneys, Lizzie entered service at the Hughes home, carrying only a satchel. She turned to tip a porter, who delivered Kate's trunk. A haughty man in butler uniform appeared in the entrance. "Miss Katie Logan?"

Lizzie said: "Yes!"

Butler said: "Welcome to the Hughes home. You come highly recommended by the Widneys. I am reassured by your reference letters from Mr. Farmer and Mrs. Widney. We'll need your services for about a week while our regular maid is on vacation."

❧ ❧

The following week, with a porter struggling (again) behind her with Kate Morgan's trunk, Lizzie entered the servants' entrance of the L. A. Grants' home at 917 South Hill Street, Los Angeles. It was mid-November 1892. She was used to her impersonation by now, and very glad to have some employment and the income. Being on short term meant that you got paid weekly, and she relished the idea of having some cash around. She met Mr. Grant, a contractor, and Mrs. Grant. They liked Lizzie very much from the first. Mrs. Grant told her at the start: "We've had glowing reports about you from the Widneys and the Hugheses, Katie, as well as Mr. Farmer's letter. What a refined and lovely young woman you are."

Lizzie said: "Thank you. I'll do my best for you."

Mr. Grant said: "I'm sure you will. And with Thanksgiving coming later this month, I'm sure you will have fun helping prepare a wonderful dinner."

Lizzie said: "I look forward to it. Thank you."

She began to feel more pregnant. One day, as she swept a carpeted parlor with a rolling sweeper, Lizzie held her stomach and ran from the room. After vomiting in the bathroom, she returned to her work and grimaced with stomach cramps. Just then, another maid walked through, carrying a stack of towels, and saw her grimace. "Hello, Katie. Everything okay?"

Lizzie said: "Yes. A little touch of something—I ate something funny last night."

"That'll do it every time."

After the maid left, Lizzie broke down crying. She took out her hankie and quietly sobbed for a while. Then she reminded herself that Kate Morgan was helping her in so many ways. She dreamed of living with John Longfield, and what a wonderful time they would have together.

The very next day, Lizzie and the other maid grabbed lunch in the kitchen on a short break. As they ate, they jabbered in random conversation. The other maid said: "...so I had this Uncle Wilbur who never liked his name, and all the kids called him Willie..."

Lizzie said: "...Some names are like that. My mother's name is Elizabeth, which is also my real name, which is why everyone calls me Lizzie..."

The other maid sat gaping at her with eyes wide open.

Lizzie froze, realizing she had made a huge mistake. "I'm joking, of course. Actually, I like the name Kitty. I mean, Katie. That's what I prefer people to call me—Katie Logan."

The other maid had not yet resumed chewing, but stared at Lizzie puzzled and unconvinced. "I see. How interesting." It was an incident she would tell a Los Angeles newspaper reporter a few weeks later, but Lizzie would not know that.

The incident so shook Lizzie that she did finally contact Kate Morgan, and they met on a street corner in Los Angeles. Lizzie said: "I'm lonely. I can't do this anymore. I miss John, and I feel like a hollow person, being someone other than myself."

Kate said: "You've done swell. You feel ready to go to Coronado?"

"Yes. Let's get it all over with." She began to cry. "I want John to come spend a day with me. Why has he not been here to see me?"

Kate said: "I sent him to my home town in Iowa—to talk with my old high school friend Allen, who is the banker there, so you'll have bank credit available if you need it at the Hotel del Coronado."

Lizzie said: "Can I see my John?"

Kate said: "Of course. He'll be on the train from Denver Thanksgiving Day, and he'll go to San Diego with me. If you want, you can meet him at the Hotel Brewster in San Diego before you go to Coronado."

Lizzie dried her tears with one of her embroidered hankies. "I want to see him before that. I want to see him now."

"But honey, he's not even in California." Kate scribbled on a piece of paper and said: "The whole thing will be over in a few days, and we'll all have our money, and you'll have your man. Try to keep your act together for a few more days. Can you do that?"

Lizzie nodded. "I'm sorry. I'll pull myself together. I'm putting my complete trust in you, Kate. My life."

"I won't let you down, sweetheart." She handed Lizzie the piece of paper. "Here is the address of the Hotel Brewster at Fourth and C in San Diego. I wrote it all down for you. Go there and ask for Dr. and Mrs. M. C. Anderson. That's John and me. You're going to the Brewster to pick up the medicine to fix your problem."

Lizzie took the paper and hugged her impulsively.

Kate said: "You've been very brave. You'll have a lot of money, both of you. He'll figure out how to take care of his dumpy wife and kids so you two can make a new life together."

Lizzie dabbed at her eyes with her hankie. "Oh God, that would be divine. You think he still loves me?"

Kate said: "He loves you very much and wants to marry you. He told me so last week before he left for Iowa. He also went to Cleveland to set up a General Delivery address so his wife will think he's looking for work there. He won't even give her a real address where she can reach him."

Lizzie said: "Sounds like he'll leave her then, after all."

"He can't love her much if he won't tell her where he's staying."

Lizzie said: "Will you be there in San Diego?"

"I have to stay out of sight, Lizzie. You'll be watched by Spreckels' people. We can't afford a flub. I'm giving it five days, no more. It won't be weeks like it's been here."

Lizzie uttered a gush of relief. "Oh, good."

Kate said: "I'll send my demand to Spreckels in San Francisco by telegram. Thanksgiving is around the corner, and I expect he'll be with his family. That's a Thursday. Too far away to look in on us, and right where we want him, remembering how dear his wife and children are to him. You start taking your medicines on Thursday. Take a dose Friday, and another on Saturday. That should do the trick. Watch how it goes. If you don't have bleeding and contractions, take a fourth dose on Sunday. That will surely do the trick. If I don't give you the signal, you have your abortion right in the main lobby of his hotel. John and I will take you away, saying he is Doctor Anderson, and everything will be swell."

Lizzie said: "But no money."

Kate said: "Not in that case. But I don't think that will happen. I'll send my threat, and he'll pay up quickly to be rid of us."

Lizzie said: "Sounds scary."

"Just don't think about it," Kate said. "You'll be sick a few days, and you'll miscarry. You'll soon get better, I promise. John would kill me if anything happened to you."

"I would feel much better if I knew you were right near me. Please!"

Kate said: "Very well, then let's do this. John and I will join you at the hotel late Thursday or early Friday. We will check in as Dr. and Mrs. M. C. Anderson. You can remember that name—it's your aunt in Grand Rapids, Louisa Anderson. M is for money, and C is for can-do. You can do this, and you will have your money. We will be staying right there in the hotel with you, but you must not let on, and you must not talk to us, because I expect Spreckels' detectives will be watching you."

Lizzie said: "And—?"

Kate said: "They'll be watching if you are acting alone, or if you have accomplices—us. We want them to think you really are Charlotte Barnard, and pay out the money. If they see you have accomplices, they'll know it's a false paternity charge, and they'll have the police arrest us all. Have courage, Lizzie—trust me—it will all turn out for the best."

❧ ❧

In the early morning on November 23, Lizzie rose at the Grants' house. She dressed, went downstairs, and mingled with the other help over coffee and breakfast in the kitchen. Then she wandered into the garden by the servants' quarters. Mrs. Grant, who really liked her, waved. "Oh, there you are, Katie. So nice to see you. I want to be sure you will help Cook stuff the turkey this evening."

Lizzie whirled, looking pained. "Oh, Mrs. Grant, you are so good to me. I have to run an errand. I'm afraid it is a personal matter. I will be gone all afternoon, with your permission, but I promised to be back before dark."

Mrs. Grant said sternly: "Of course, my dear. You do what you must. But promise you'll be here to help, and I'll make sure you get a nice plate tomorrow, and some pie."

Lizzie said: "I do promise! I do so promise! Thank you!"

Lightly dressed, and carrying only a hand satchel, Lizzie wandered up and down the station platform in Los Angeles. It was late Wednesday, Nov. 23, 1892. She had already missed her promised return to help the cook stuff the turkey, and she regretted having lied to Mrs. Grant, who was so nice to her, but she was on a mission that even Kate Morgan had not sanctioned. She was going to meet John Longfield and propose that he make a commitment to marry her.

She took the train south, and got off in Santa Ana. At the ticket booths, she bought a fare east to Barstow. As she waited on the platform, she ate a sandwich and a banana, and drank coffee.

She took the train to Barstow. She rode through the night, a forlorn figure. In Barstow, Lizzie sat alone on the platform, in the dark, as November 24, 1892 rolled around—Thanksgiving Day. She knew she cut a solitary and desolate figure in the middle of nowhere, a ruined woman, gambling desperately with all her life on the two people who could save her—Kate Morgan and John Longfield. She was tired, but she was so tense that her body felt as if shot through with electricity, so she dozed only fitfully.

Night turned to morning, and still she sat there. As dawn broke, she bought coffee and buttered marmalade rolls from the station snack window when it finally opened. With her stomach somewhat full, she dozed again. And she walked up and down the platform.

At last! Midmorning, the train from Denver pulled in, and she boarded. As the train chugged southwest toward Orange and Santa Ana, Lizzie walked down the aisles of rocking coaches looking for John. Reluctantly, she put her glasses on. When she spotted Longfield, who did not see her at first, she hid her glasses in her purse, and ran to him. "John!"

"My God! Lizzie! What on earth?"

She sat by him. "I am so glad to see you." She grasped his hand,

and put her cheek on his shoulder. "I have missed you so, my love."

John said awkwardly: "This is quite a surprise."

"Are you glad to see me?"

"Yes, of course. Just tired. Been traveling for days."

Lizzie took off her jacket and rolled it up. "I understand. Here is a pillow for you."

"Thanks. What a surprise."

Lizzie said: "Do you have the three baggage receipts for my trunks?"

"Yes." He started to reach into his pocket for them, but Lizzie shook her head and said: "Keep them until we get to San Diego. It's a few hours yet. I'll take care of you. You sleep, and we'll travel to San Diego together."

Looking oddly at her, John put his head on her jacket by the window, and fell asleep. Lizzie sat patiently watching the landscape roll by, lost in her thoughts and dreams. She dozed a bit herself, being overly tired.

At some point, someone said: "We're almost there." People began to take down their luggage, close their sandwich boxes, get ready to disembark. Lizzie shook John. A sign passed: *Orange 10 Miles*. Lizzie said: "We're almost on the West Coast, darling. Wake up."

John stirred. He yawned and wiped his eyes. He blinked repeatedly as he saw her, as if he could not believe he was seeing her there.

Lizzie thought she read coldness and resentment in his gaze, but pushed the feeling away because it couldn't be. It mustn't be. It would mean the end of the world. She said: "Kate told me you and she will sign into the Hotel del Coronado as Dr. and Mrs. Anderson."

"That's new to me, Lizzie. Don't go changing the plan now."

"I'm not changing the plan, John. Kate did. She's in charge."

"Yeah, that's right. Well..." He waggled a finger. "Lizzie, I'm not going to San Diego with you."

"You're not?" She felt thunderstruck.

"We can't be seen together. Remember Kate said that?"

"Oh yes." She remembered, but something wasn't right here. They sat in silence for a few minutes. "Kate said you went to Cleveland."

"That's right. Cleveland."

"To mail your wife some news," Lizzie prodded. *I hope you sent her a letter saying you want a divorce*, she thought. He seemed so odd coldly distant...unloving... Lizzie grew alarmed again. She was tired, and scared, and trusting—could he not understand that she needed some reassurance?

"I don't want her to know where I am."

She put her hands together in his lap, over his hands. "You don't love her anymore." It was a statement, a question, a plea. She needed him to love her. Enough of the pretense. She wanted him for herself. It had to be that way. She was carrying his child, which she was willing to abort for him according to Kate Morgan's plan, so that Lizzie and John could be together. So why was he now being evasive? Did he not love her? Her heart would break if he did not love her.

John ignored her hands and said: "What? What makes you say I don't love her? I love you, Lizzie. I told you not to think too much ahead." He pulled his hands away as if out of a bear trap.

"If you love me, then leave her and marry me." She crossed her hands over her aching and scared heart, sitting bolt upright like a scared rabbit.

"I have children, Lizzie. I'm tired—stop joking around. "

Lizzie said: "I was hoping—"

"Nothing is simple or easy, Lizzie."

"You're just tired, John. I'm tired. Neither of us is making any sense."

"You know that I like you very much—"

Lizzie said: "You like me very much. You like donuts or beer very much. What does it mean? I am willing to give you my life. I am carrying your child. Do you love me as I love you?"

John said: "One of my children is sick, I am told, and people say my wife is looking haggard. I worry about them. Yes, I worry about you too. I love you. I love all of you. I have no time to love myself with all this damned loving."

Lizzie said: "So you really have no thoughts of being with me. It's the money you want. I am your pregnant mistress, a ruined woman, and you tell me you are worried about your wife and children. Am I supposed to give a damn about everyone else in the world at this point?"

John said: "Lizzie, you'll drive us both crazy with this talk. We agreed to just think about the next few days, get through this thing at the hotel."

A sallow man in a black suit became aware of their conversation as their voices rose. He watched the developing spat with the bored attentiveness of a traveler trapped in the moment. He would tell a bellman some time later, who would tell newspaper reporters.

As the train approached Orange, Lizzie was in tears. She could not afford to lose him. She was desperate. "I am sorry. I'll do whatever you want me to. Please, John—"

John felt himself grow inarticulate. "You drive me crazy babbling so."

Lizzie sobbed. "I'm sorry. I know you are going to leave me. Please don't do it, because I will die. Don't leave me. Please."

"I'm sorry I got myself into this. I can't sleep nights for worry."

Lizzie said: "About me? Or about yourself?"

John yelled: "About you. About me. About my wife. About each of my kids, whom I love." The train ground to a stop, and John rose.

Lizzie tugged at his jacket, but he darted down the aisle. Lizzie wailed: "Please! Don't leave me! I'm sorry."

John bounded off the train in a panic and ran, dodging left and right through the thick crowd. He vanished in two or three minutes.

The sallow man, whose name was Joseph Jones, rose and followed Lizzie off the train. He too was headed for the Hotel del Coronado that day. He would be amazed to see her again in the lobby of the Hotel del Coronado as they both registered. He would avoid direct involvement in the great mystery that was about to grip the entire United States through breathless hour by hour telegraphic reports to the Yellow Press. But he would tell reporters about the man and woman he'd seen on the train. For over a century, people would be puzzled how a girl who was on her way south from Los Angeles to San Diego could simultaneously be on a train headed west from Denver to the coast at Orange and Santa Ana. That it would take her an entire day to make a two-hour train trip from Los Angeles to San Diego, from the time she left the Grants to her signing in at the Hotel del Coronado the following afternoon would be remembered as a mystery within a mystery—the so-called Missing Day. The case that was about to break would be a national sensation for weeks, and an enigma full of tantalizing and contradictory clues for many generations.

8. Conspiracy—Late Autumn 1892

The old Spreckels Mansion in San Francisco resided on well-kept, green grounds on a slope overlooking the bay and harbor entrance leading to the Pacific Ocean. In the working wing of the building, a messenger hurried down office corridors that clattered with typing. Male secretaries and female typists came and went through office doors, but many offices were empty because of the Thanksgiving holiday. The messenger moved along Mahogany Row, the executive section, to a door with the name *Mr. John Spreckels* on it. Another door had a sign reading *Mr. Spreckels' Secretary*.

The messenger knocked on the secretarial door. A demure, well-dressed female receptionist in her 40s opened the door. Seeing the messenger's uniform and satchel, she let him into a carpeted office suite. The messenger had been here before, and knocked on the main door. An older man's gruff voice called out inside: "Yes, come in."

Inside the room, the messenger found a balding man of about 60 working at a desk. Joshua Babbitt had been one of the Spreckels' chief adjutants for many years. The messenger handed over a sealed envelope. "Priority telegram, Sir—highly personal for Mr. Spreckels."

"Thanks," said the secretary, handing him a tip. The messenger nodded and left, and the secretary opened the telegram. His eyes bulged and his jaw dropped as he read the message from a Lottie Bernard in San Diego. This woman claimed to have worked for John Spreckels as a domestic. Her tone was unseemly and familiar. She wrote that she had a stack of incriminating love letters. Not only that, but she said she was pregnant with John Spreckels' child, and required a large sum of money to discreetly raise the child and cause Mr. Spreckels no further anxiety. In other words, she was blackmailing him under threat of causing him a terrible embarrassment—at his hotel in Coronado, at the worst possible moment. Did this woman realize that John Spreckels was at that moment sitting opposite President Benjamin Harrison in the White House, in tense negotiations for the future of the Spreckels sugar plantations in Hawai'i, the future of that nation itself, and to a considerable extent the future of capitalism in the United States? Was she just naïve, or a genius who understood the growing hunger of corporate America to create overseas empires in Central and South America as well as Hawai'i? Not to mention the decaying Spanish empire around the world? Her timing just had to be a diabolical coincidence. There was also the possibility that Spreckels' enemies were planting a scandal, framing John, to hurt his father, and deal a fatal blow to their chances of holding on to Hawai'i. *Dreadful. Just dreadful.* Babbitt rose and hurried to a mahogany door leading into the private offices of John Spreckels; his brother Adolph; and their father Claus, head of the dynasty of Sugar Barons. Those offices were, at the moment, quiet and nearly empty. Even the air was almost devoid of its constant pall of cigar smoke, and servants had opened the windows to let in fresh air. John was in Washington D.C. lobbying the President and Congress. Claus, the dynasty's founder, was in Honolulu for desperate, last-minute shuttle diplomacy to stave off an imminent coup against Queen Lili'uokalani and her government. Adolph was away on business somewhere. That left an Executive Vice President and Chief of Operations, Peter Maurice, in charge of the Spreckels business empire.

Maurice and Babbitt stood together reading. "The nerve!" said Secretary Babbitt.

"She must be crazy," EVP Maurice said: "Not a word of this to anyone."

"Of course, Mr. Maurice, understood. Anything I can do to help out?"

Maurice thought for a moment, rattling the telegram in one hand to help focus his anger into strategy. "Get me the cipher code book. This is an outrage. How dare this woman? I'll immediately telegraph Mr. Spreckels and the Pinkertons in Washington, D. C."

"And the hotel in Coronado?"

"Let's let Mr. Spreckels decide how he wants to handle this. I will advise him to let the Pinkertons handle this from the start, since this is one of their specialties—high-stakes blackmail."

In the Oval Office, President Benjamin Harrison and John Spreckels were conferring. Harrison was a white-haired, bearded man of quiet disposition and slight frame. Spreckels, in his thirties and just graying slightly, was handsome and carried himself with the natural ease and dignity of one born into financial princeliness. He was just concluding a line of persuasive argument: "Mr. President, I hope to bring together some of our party in Congress to effect a consensus."

President Harrison said: "Mr. Spreckels, certainly I oppose any sort of imperialistic move to annex a sovereign nation. Much as Hawai'i looks tempting, going that far would make us look bad."

"I have no illusions," Spreckels said. "They'll do it in increments so the world won't notice. It's the snake strategy. I've watched a boa constrictor crush its victim, and then devour it slowly, one heaving gulp at a time." President Harrison grimaced. Both men were Republicans, supporters of industry and big business. They felt comfortable with each other as they teased and argued back and forth. The problem, as Spreckels saw it, was that his father's rivals had more support in the Republican-dominated Senate, and even in the Democratically led House of the 52nd Congress. Spreckels said: "The Missionary Party and the Dole interests are creating popular sentiment in the national press here in the United States. They are portraying the Hawai'ian people and their beautiful crown princess as monkeys and cannibals, to turn the American people against them, and to cause our people to support annexation."

President Harrison said: "I agree, it's a nasty business. But Mr. Spreckels, allow me to play Devil's Advocate for a moment. The question before us is—should I, as President, intervene in a matter between corporate rivals? After all, your father owns most of the cane fields in that nation. He controls the government through his friendship with the royal family. He has amassed a great fortune in sugar—a virtual monopoly—while other U.S. corporations seek to gain a foothold and generate profits. That is the narrow line I must tread here. The Dole faction will argue that what's good for business is good for America, and that preserving the Spreckels monopoly on sugar is not in our nation's best interests."

Spreckels said more heatedly: "Mr. Dole and his pineapple

monopoly are thriving, so it seems clear to me that they don't need to overthrow the legitimate government of Hawai'i..."

Someone knocked on the door, and President Harrison said: "Come in."

A male secretary stepped in. "Mr. President, excuse me. There is an extremely urgent visitor for Mr. Spreckels, on a personal matter."

Spreckels immediately blanched, thinking there might have been a death in the family. President Harrison told Spreckels with kind sympathy: "Go on—I'll go have lunch. We can reconvene this afternoon. We still have much to talk about."

Spreckels rose. "My deepest apologies, Mr. President." He followed the secretary out of the room and into the hallway outside.

As John Spreckels stepped out of the President's office, the male secretary waved close a man in a business suit. The man waited until the secretary stepped away, then introduced himself. "My name is Desmond Pinkerton. I'm a second cousin and employee of Alan Pinkerton, the founder of our agency. I'm here on a mission of special urgency, requested by your offices in San Francisco in the absence of you and your father. They received a telegram, addressed to you personally, which is being treated with the utmost sensitivity and secrecy, I assure you. It will be best if you read this telegraphic transcript of what they received in San Francisco." With that, he handed over a sealed document, which Spreckels tore open and read. In seconds, Spreckels had grasped the situation. "This is blackmail, pure and simple," he told Pinkerton as he felt blood pounding in his temples. He remembered Charlotte Barnard all too well. A beautiful young woman, and very discreet, except that his wife hated her instinctively. His wife, Lillie, suspected he had affairs here and there. They were an adventurous family, all the Spreckelses, but you had to play it smart. Lillie had fired the girl for ineptitude, and John had paid her off generously. How was it possible she was now blackmailing him?

Pinkerton nodded. "Of course."

Spreckels said: "I'm overloaded with important matters. I can hardly add this to my list of urgent concerns. And yet this woman wants to ruin my reputation, and she could destroy the work I am here to do."

"Of course, Mr. Spreckels. This distraction needs to be handled by competent service. We are quite experienced in dealing with situations like this. If you want to employ me, I will trouble you very little with it. I have only one concern."

Spreckels said: "What is it?"

"This young woman has checked in at your hotel in Coronado. She claims to be the mother of your child, if you will forgive me for voicing such an outrage."

Spreckels turned red and trembled, with a look of distress and shame. "I should have known."

Pinkerton nodded. "The name she gives is Lottie A. Bernard. Does this name have any resonance with you?"

Spreckels said: "Oh the devil, yes, I might as well come clean to you, though I'll deny anything—"

"No need to worry. I give you the seal of the confessional. I will take your secrets to my grave. We are Pinkertons, after all."

"I work hard, and I love my family. As you can imagine, a man of my standing is surrounded by temptation, and I am generally very disciplined. I don't make a habit of womanizing. But, as it happened, circumstances being what they were for a brief time, I had an unfortunate and thoughtless liaison with a domestic named Charlotte Barnard earlier this year. It was a foolish mistake on my part."

"Did you exchange any letters with her, as this woman claims?"

"Love notes, I am ashamed to say. I never signed them, but they are in my handwriting."

Pinkerton said: "The woman says she is willing to sell them to you, in effect. Would you consider paying the sum she asks?"

Spreckels said: "What a nuisance! I paid her off and sent her packing. She didn't strike me as a copperhead."

"People can be two-faced. Or desperate."

"What if she keeps a few letters and comes back with it later? She could sell them to a newspaper—"

"We can plant some rumors. Trust me, we are very good at this. I'll assume she has more duplicity planned, and we'll tactically and strategically anticipate her and outflank her. There are a number of what-ifs here, and we can anticipate most of them. The key is to neutralize her, pay her off again, and blacken her reputation so she cannot credibly cause any more scandal."

Spreckels said: "Thanks! Please deal with this for me. I will pay whatever fees you require, gladly."

"Might you really have impregnated this woman? Think carefully."

Spreckels deliberated. "Depends how far along she is. I last saw Charlotte late summer. Sadly, yes, it's possible. The timing would be just right. It's November, and she'd be about four months along."

"Let's not draw any conclusions," Pinkerton said with calm assurance. "If she has any accomplices down there in Coronado, it's a closed case—she would be a fake. We are quite used to dealing with these situations."

Spreckels said: "What do you suggest?"

Pinkerton said: "Our rule of thumb is quite simple and usually effective. If the girl is acting alone, pay her and get her out of your hair. If she has accomplices, then she clearly is a simple blackmailer. We'll have a different approach, and it has to be done carefully— discredit them, counter their lies with lies of our own, so that they lose all credibility. We usually spread stories that they are grifters, cardsharps, gypsies, that sort of thing. They'll seem quite repulsive when our stories get into the popular press."

Relieved, Spreckels said. "You'll handle it then? You feel you can?"

Pinkerton nodded. "We'll have our local talent in San Diego shadow this woman, see how far along she is, and make a judgment on that if possible. We'll see if she has accomplices—if not, pay her off, get the documents from her, search her room and her belongings for any other letters, and be done with it. If she has accomplices, we bring in the police and round up the whole gang. We then orchestrate a clean-up so that anything they say will make them sound worse than they already are. If any other notes surface, we'll bring in experts who will testify they are fakes."

Spreckels said: "Very well then. My man in San Francisco was right to bring you in. We can't afford embarrassment at this moment. Even my own agents in San Diego must not know anything about this."

Pinkerton said: "I send out telegrams instantly. We are already hard at work, and will resolve the matter for you very quickly."

9. San Diego—November 1892

Around noon on Thanksgiving Day—November 24, 1892—Lizzie Wyllie arrived in San Diego. Still reeling from her disastrous meeting with John Longfield on the train from Denver to the coast, she was a pale face sitting at the window as the southbound train from Santa Ana huffed and chuffed into San Diego's 1887 California Southern Railway train station. The small but ornate wooden station, which was square and had on top a disproportionately large clock tower, was full of people coming and going. San Diego had blossomed into a city of over 45,000 during the brief boom of the 1880s. The economy collapsed back to fewer than 20,000 souls trying to eke out a living after the panic of 1889. Speculation had driven the real estate and financial markets through the roof—most notably, that the Santa Fe Railroad was about to push through a direct artery of the Transcontinental Railroad, which proved to be untrue. Also, initial enthusiasm about French efforts to build a canal through Panama had also killed the idea of San Diego as an important cargo hub—though by 1892, after more than 20,000 worker deaths, total failure of the French venture was imminent, due to poor planning, virulent tropical diseases, and seemingly impossible geological and hydrological problems. San Diego's real estate and financial ventures collapsed overnight, and one could buy land for pennies on the dollar—if one wanted to live in this beautiful but isolated and impoverished place. Much of the Spanish and Mexican Old Town at the mouth of Mission Valley had burned down in the early 1870s, about the same time that Connecticut newcomer Alonzo Horton developed his New City on nearly 1,000 acres of beachfront land on San Diego Bay. The military saw San Diego's harbor as one of the finest natural harbors on the Pacific Coast. Entrepreneurs Hampton Story and Elisha Babcock had developed Coronado Island. They'd built the Hotel del Coronado in 1887 as a fabulous red-turreted fantasy resort, opening in February 1888. After the collapse of '89, John Spreckels bought up everything in sight—North Island and South Island, the newspapers, the utilities, the light rail, banks, even the open flume that brought water from the East County mountains to this arid coastal city. The Depression of 1893 was yet to strike, and San Diego, in 1892, was still a shattered ghost of its glorious past decade, sleeping in the sunlight.

This was the moment in time, and the place, in which Lizzie Wyllie got off the train and pretended to be the imaginary person named Lottie Anderson Bernard. It was the start of her lethal adventure at the Hotel del Coronado.

Still shaken from the ill-omened meeting with her lover John Longfield, she went from the train station next door to the baggage terminal. At a window, she addressed a red-faced older man in a gray smock and dark blue cap. "Sir, I have come to collect my three trunks."

The baggage agent said gruffly without looking at her: "Got your checks?"

Lizzie said: "No, my husband has them, and he got off in Santa Ana."

The rude man said: "Have him come pick them up then."

Lizzie said: "I don't know how to contact him, and I need my dresses and shoes and things. Everything I own is in those trunks."

"You have no business here." It was the social custom that a young single women must travel with either her husband, a male relative, or an older female chaperone. The baggage man regarded her as if she were a woman of ill repute. "Someone with you?"

Lizzie said: "I'm not traveling alone by my choice. Look, my name is—"

"I don't care what your name is. Rules are rules, girlie. No checks, no baggage. Now get lost." He slammed the window shut on her. Distraught, she turned away.

Lizzie remembered that Kate Morgan had said she could meet her and John at a hotel. She found the address in her purse, written in Kate's handwriting. After asking directions of a woman waiting for a train, Lizzie walked east on C Street. Her walk took her into Alonzo Horton's New City. Some of the buildings she passed, like the back of Horton's grand hotel, reminded her of the big buildings in a real city. This felt like a backward little town trying to become a great city like Detroit or Chicago. The streets were neatly named, with letters running east-west and numbers running north-south.

At Fourth and C, Lizzie saw the splendid, wood-and-stucco Hotel Brewster, several stories high, which occupied the entire city block. It was a large modern hotel offering clean rooms, safety, and comfort to traveling businessmen. In the spacious lobby, she made her way across shining wood floors and area rugs to the front desk. There she addressed a male concierge. "Sir, I am looking for my brother and his wife."

The concierge, a tall, dark-haired young man in a black suit, asked: "Are they guests here, Miss?"

"They said they'd be here—Dr. M.C. Anderson and his wife Louisa."

"Let me see if they checked in." He spent a minute or two looking at the guest register on the marble counter top. "No, I'm sorry, there is nobody by that name registered here. I didn't think they sounded familiar."

Lizzie felt stung—puzzled, and mortified. What next? Was everything meant to go wrong? Seeing her consternation, the man said, "Wait here a moment," and went to speak with a tall, dark-haired woman at a counter nearby. She seemed to be an authority figure in her black silk dress, with a severe looking silver and mother-of-pearl brooch over one breast. The dark woman approached with the concierge. Lizzie regarded the woman with an instinctive mix of hope and dread. The woman had a strong, deep voice. "Are you looking for a Dr. Anderson and his wife?"

Lizzie said: "Yes!"

"What is your name?"

Lizzie said: "Mrs. Lottie Anderson Bernard."

"Follow me." She led Lizzie into an office marked *Assistant Manager*. She closed the door. "Sit down, please." The woman seemed a bit scary to Lizzie, sort of veiled and dark-minded. Her features were handsome, if one could say as much, not unpleasant. She was attractive without losing a certain forbidding air. Or maybe it was a touch of evil. Lizzie knew she did not read people well, especially without her glasses. She sat down before the desk, and the tall woman went to a cupboard. She took out a small package and placed it before Lizzie. Then she sat down behind the desk. "Examine it and see if it is what you came for."

Lizzie opened it with trembling fingers and found a little cardboard box. In it was a vial of medicine with a note rolled around it and held by an elastic. The note read: *If the pain gets too bad, see the doctor*. It was signed simply *Druggist*.

Lizzie said: "What is this?"

The tall woman said: "Dr. and Mrs. Anderson came to see me and left that for you. They said you would know what to do with it. Your medicine. I know nothing more. I don't know who those two people really were. They paid me a small sum, to be sure and give you this package when you came asking for them." She nodded, looking at the box. "There's my end of the bargain."

Lizzie slipped the box into her purse. In a shaky voice, she said: "I was hoping to speak with them. She said to ask for them here."

The tall woman shook her head vehemently, and rose. "We're done, I'm afraid. This feels like shady business, and I want no more part of it. Good day, Lottie, and best of luck to you." Her expression was pitying.

❧ ❧

In an office in the Pinkerton building in San Diego sat two long-term, trusted Pinkerton employees. They had a wooden desk between them, and a filing cabinet and other amenities around them in the second floor office that would be the operating headquarters for the case.

Senior Special Detective Jeb Collins was briefing subordinate Special Detective Sam Dolbee on the case. Dolbee lived and worked in San Diego, while Collins was an expert who had been rushed down from Los Angeles. "We are the only two men in San Diego who will be fully inside on the case. The client's name will remain secret from the rest of our Pinkerton people, from the local police, and even from Spreckels' personal detectives at the banks and hotels."

Detective Sam Dolbee finishing reading the case file as he listened. "That's quite a situation." He closed the folder and handed it back.

Senior Detective Collins put the case file in a large safe and locked its door. Dolbee said: "You say she is at the Hotel del Coronado?"

Collins said: "Yes. Just got the information via telegram from Washington, and confirmed it by telephone with the hotel desk. It seems clear that she's at his hotel to blackmail him."

"What's the procedure typically?" Dolbee asked.

"It's simple. We need to find out if she is really pregnant, and acting alone and in desperation, or if she is just a criminal. The way we determine that is if we find accomplices involved."

Dolbee nodded. "Seems reasonable."

Collins continued: "Spreckels doesn't want his personal army involved. I gather he owns all of Coronado, most of San Diego, and much of San Diego County." Dolbee well knew that the city was still a backwater with no detective force of their own—they'd only recently started up a small uniformed police department. The mayor's office and the police headquarters were in a brownstone overlooking the edge of the Stingaree, the second biggest and craziest red light district on the West Coast after the one in Frisco. The U.S. Frontier had just been declared officially gone by the national census of 1890. The approximately twenty lawless blocks were a remaining patch of the great Wild West, and its most famous inhabitant was none other than Wyatt Earp. The retired Frontier lawman now ran four gambling saloons, and raced fine horses in Del Mar.

Dolbee suggested: "I would ask Wyatt Earp to help lend a hand. He's a little shady, but he's still a lawman at heart, and he might work with us if we need."

Collins nodded. "I'll buy that. Can you get a hold of him quickly? Will he be discreet?"

"Sure. I know the guy. I now how he works. He's quiet, and doesn't miss a thing. We just need to ask him to look out for any signs of unusual activity involving the Hotel del Coronado. Strange people moving through the Stingaree, without seeming to belong. Sooner or later, every shady character in the region filters through his casinos."

"That's right," Collins said heartily. "Amateurs just give themselves away. They skulk around with a dark cloud over their heads like a billboard."

"Any other instructions?" Dolbee asked.

" I'll direct the other agents without telling them the full picture. Time is short. We need to shadow her every move at the Hotel del Coronado for signs of accomplices. I'm having other staff watch the train station and the hotels, and any other logical points of passage for signs of anything unusual. We'll make this room our headquarters, and then as quickly as possible figure out all we can about her. Nobody is to set foot in here but you and me. If she's knocked up legit, we pay her and run her out of town. If she's part of a gang, we lock them up, keep the press away, and spread rumors about them so nobody will believe anything they say, just in case the story gets out. If we can, make a deal—freedom to leave town rather than jail time if they clam up."

Dolbee said: "I'll get to the Hotel Del quick as I can."

"Just a minute." Collins rose and walked to a large black steel safe. "I've been given some cash for field operations. There is no time to lose, and we can use whatever sum we need. Spreckels will pay any price." He spun the dials and unlocked the safe. There, amid stacks of important papers, sat a tidy block of paper money in various denominations. He took a few fives off the top and handed them to Dolbee. "This will keep you flush as you get started. If you need bribe money or anything, just let me know. Spreckels will pay anything to keep this hushed up."

John and Kate stayed in a small, cheap hotel near the waterfront in San Diego, on India near Date. They had registered as Douglas and Claire Lomax. Kate put their lone large open suitcase under the window for easy access. They had little baggage between them. Kate's trunk still sat in the L. A. Grant house in Los Angeles. The trunk would be safe there. She could send for it later, pretending to be Katie Logan, and apologize that her mother was dying and it had proven impossible for her to return.

John and Kate sat on the bed, eating ham and cheese sandwiches with pickles and beer. They both felt relaxed and content, letting Lizzie take the brunt of risk.

John said: "It's a bit boring, this waiting."

Kate produced a few dollars. "Johnny, I know you want to go have yourself a beer and watch the ladies. Just stay away from the card tables."

He took the money, counted it, kissed it, and put it in his trouser pocket. "Bless you, my darling. What a golden woman you are."

Kate said: "Relax. Have a beer or two. Clear your mind. Let me do the thinking. Stay low, don't attract any attention." She grinned. "I'm going to go have my hair done. It helps me think."

≈ ≈

On her way to the hairdresser, Kate walked by the Hotel Brewster. She walked along the building on its Fifth Street side, and tossed a small pebble at a first-floor window. The window opened, and the tall woman in dark clothing leaned out.

Kate said: "Did she come by?"

"Yes. I gave her the medicine as you said." Her voice was low and full.

"Did she seem okay? How was she taking things?"

The tall woman said: "She seemed pitiful. She looked tired and nervous, and she almost cried when I told her you two aren't here."

Kate handed her a five dollar bill. "Thanks. Here is the rest. Our business is finished."

The tall woman folded her money quickly and closed the window.

Kate headed south on Fifth Street, looking for the hairdresser shop to which someone at the hotel had referred her. Along the way, she noticed a mustachioed man leaning on a porch, chewing a toothpick and casually watching the street. He wore a six-shooter under his jacket. His eyes caught Kate's attention—they had the razor-sharp glint of a lawman's penetrating gaze, but she saw no badge. He looked like a tough customer, and made Kate a bit nervous. The law was no friend of hers.

Kate walked into the hairdresser's and got herself situated in a hair trimming chair attended by a buxom woman in her forties, who never stopped talking. Kate tried to ignore her, and watched people outside through the window. She saw the mustachioed man loitering about as if he were looking for someone. Kate had a touch of paranoia about Tom Morgan, and this man stirred ominous, sinister feelings in her. The hair cutter noticed her looking, and said: "You're interested in that buckaroo over there, eh?"

"Just curious," Kate said.

"You know who that is?" She waited a second, stopped clipping and combing, and then said with a flourish: "That's Wyatt Earp."

Kate was genuinely surprised. "No." Her instinctive alarm deepened.

"Yes. He runs several gambling saloons and race horses here in town. His place is over in the Stingaree, if you know the Yuma

Building."

"Not really. I'm new in town."

"Well, you'd do well to stay away from there. Avoid the streets between 1st and 6th, and between H and K. So are you going to be in town long?"

"I'm just here on business with my husband."

"Oh? What business is your husband in?"

"He imports and exports beer."

"Oh? You mean like in business establishments?"

"Yes, exactly."

"Where does the beer come from?"

"Usually not far away. Mostly local. Sometimes fancy, from far away."

"Sounds exciting."

"He does get excited about it."

"Your husband must do a brisk business."

"He does." Kate thought to herself, stifling a laugh as she thought, *He imports it all right—from the table, to the toilet. Why does this busybody need to ask?* She changed the subject. "So Wyatt Earp is now a gambling man?"

"He calls himself a Capitalist," she said as she continued snipping and clipping Kate's thick hair. "I think he works both sides of the law, personally. A lot of coppers do. Just look at them crooks over in the Stingaree, with City Hall and the Police Headquarters overlooking the whole crazy sing-along by night and by day."

After about an hour, when Kate's hair was done—tightly curled, with a slight burned smell from the curling irons, and fragrant with pomade—she took a walk down into the Stingaree to see for herself. It was the equal of any large city red light district she had ever seen. The main body of it seemed to be a long rectangle about four blocks east-west and about eight blocks north-south. There was even a small Chinatown containing laundries, opium dens, and cat houses. The main action was in the Stingaree itself, though. On Fourth, Fifth, and Sixth Streets, Kate saw house upon house of prostitution, gambling, drinking, and any other vice you could name. The women were not allowed to leave their district, so the madams hired a corps of young men on high-wheel bicycles to come racing at all hours of the day and night with the finest wines and baskets of catered steak, lobster, and just about any fine food imaginable. Kate was curious about Earp, and found the Yuma Building on Fifth Street. It was a tall, narrow building with an ornate façade in several noisy colors. She recognized the man from a distance, by his great mustachio and sharp-eyed gaze. As she spotted him, she saw he was being tailed by a dark-suited man in a Bowler hat. The Bowler man didn't look like someone who belonged in the Stingaree. If anything, he had the hard chops and cold eyes of a detective.

Kate hung back and watched the two men. All around her were flying bottles and screaming women, caterers racing by on bicycles, gunmen riding in or out on their horses, women coming and going in carriages, and often a distant pop of gunfire and the laughter and shrieking of drugged and drunken men and women.

Earp stepped up into his gambling saloon on Fifth Street. The Bowler man, having apparently had his fill of observing Earp, took the closing door as his cue to turn and walk north on Fifth, back to the civilized part of town. Many streets here had been paved during the boom years, and each city block had a tall metal tower with a bank of electric lights high up to mimic sunlight (or at least the full moon) at night. Kate followed half a block behind. He crossed a street, and walked through an alley opening on a wide street, which he crossed. Kate stopped on the opposite sidewalk, because the Bowler had stepped inside the city's clearly marked Pinkerton headquarters. She frowned and thought: *Why is Earp being followed by these people? Could this be about me and Lizzie?* She had never pulled off a scheme this elaborate, and she began to wonder if she'd bitten off more than she could chew. But she'd always managed to charm and talk her way out of a situation, so maybe she could do it again here if necessary. She prepared herself to bolt at the first sign that Spreckels wasn't just easily sending the money.

When Kate returned to the hotel room, she found John sleeping. She took off her hat and started to nervously undress. John stirred in his sleep and muttered drunkenly. Kate said: "I thought you'd be out somewhere."

John groaned and sat up, smelling boozy. "I got side tracked at a pretty little bar, and thought I would have those beers like you said. I don't feel ready to gamble. When I feel that itch in my fingers, I'll wander over into the Stingaree and rake up a pile of dough."

Kate said: "You better sober up. I think we're in deep water here."

John said: "Why?"

Kate said: "This is a small town. I have a feeling the Spreckels people are more clever and determined than I imagined. I get these gut feelings, and right now my gut is starting to feel like a trapped animal." She explained about Earp and the man she'd followed, adding: "I'm going to think what to do next. If the money doesn't come quickly, we may just have to cut and run."

"And Lizzie?"

"We take her along if we can." She had no intention of being captured by the police or the Pinkertons if things went wrong—not to save Lizzie, nor to save John. She could not tell him this, of course. She remembered, too, that she had made one fatal mistake. She, the mistress of false names, had given John and Lizzie her real name. Now she could not simply abandon them—because they knew who she was, and it would only be a matter of time before the police were looking for her. If that happened, she could never use her real name again.

Tom Morgan was holed up in the Eagle Hotel, a tiny building on the eastern outskirts of sleepy Salem, Oregon. He'd pulled off a job with some boys up near Portland, waylaying a Wells Fargo shipment. There was supposed to be gold on board, but it turned out to be a few measly little bags of silver coins. But it was nearly a grand, and Tom managed to drive the other two boys off at gunpoint and elope with the coins, so he was flush for a little while. About once a month, he would telegraph an old friend of his back in his home town of Hamburg, Iowa, a fellow named Allen, who had known both Tom and Kate. His friend was quietly watching out for the possible reappearance in her home town of Kate Morgan, to whom Tom was still legally married. He'd curbed his drinking lately, out of regrets for losing her. He longed for her. He missed the old days when they'd ridden the trains, gambling and conning men for their money. Tom knew he wasn't any prize, but he hoped somehow that they could be together again. His years with her had been the best of his life, and he'd been a fool not to know it.

To Tom's surprise, a telegram arrived within the hour from Hamburg. It was signed Allen, and said:

> Kate in San Diego STOP + possibly at a hotel, not sure which STOP + Deposited $25 credit at bank here STOP + may claim it next few days STOP + All I know thus far + STOP.

Tom's heart skipped a beat. This was what he'd been waiting for the past few years—a chance to get on his knees and beg his wife to come back to him. He loved her very much and pined for her. Packing his suitcase in a great hurry, he rushed for the train station. He'd be in San Diego within a day or two. Oh God, he'd see his Katie Farmer again and he'd beg her to come back to him. What great times they'd had together! What great times they could have again together! Within an hour, he was on a train heading south along the California coast. When nobody was looking, he polished his twin Deringers and prepared himself inwardly for mortal combat with any man who would stand in his way. He was a desperate man, but a righteous one. The Law and the Bible were very clear on this. Kate was his lawfully wedded wife, his property, his chattel, and he had the God-given right and obligation to retrieve her, to protect her, to keep her by his side.

10. Coronado—Thanksgiving 1892

Lizzie left the Hotel Brewster after her upsetting meeting with the tall, dark woman. She took the ferry across the bay, which was a nice, sunny, breezy ride. Having been unable to retrieve her trunks, she carried only her satchel with a few things in it. She rode across the length of Coronado Island on the steam trolley, rolling down the center of Orange Avenue along the store fronts and decorative palm trees. Less than a mile and a half from the ferry landing, she stepped off the trolley before a magnificent white hotel with brick-red conical roofs and white turrets. The Hotel del Coronado lifted her spirits. The sunshine and fresh air restored her a bit. She slipped back into her wishful dream, in which John came to get her and they lived happily ever after. The hotel was a Victorian confection with no two walls, windows, turrets, or other features matching any other.

Lizzie entered the hotel's cool, shady lobby and walked to the desk. She put her satchel down and leaned her elbows on the desk. A young clerk saw her and came to help her. He looked a bit puzzled and uneasy about admitting an attractive, elegantly dressed young woman who was traveling without luggage, alone and unchaperoned. He went to consult with a frowning chief clerk, and then returned. After a brief conversation, the young man signed the guest register for her. The pen paused in his hand a second. He had started to write *Miss*. "Can you spell that for me?"

Lizzie enunciated: "Mrs. Lottie Anderson Bernard."

"Will Mr. Bernard be checking in today also?" he asked as he changed the *Miss* to *Mrs*.

Lizzie said: "No, but I expect my brother and his wife, Dr. and Mrs. M. C. Anderson, to check in later today."

"Very good, Mrs. Bernard. The bellman will see you to your room."

Another young man in his early 20s stepped forward, wearing the standard uniform of bellmen—a modified Crimean War officer's uniform with pillbox hat, all in burgundy, with gilded braiding. "My name is Harry West. I manage the third floor. Any luggage today, or does Mr. Bernard have it with him?"

There was an instant spark of platonic friendship between them. Harry wore a wedding ring and seemed innocently just a pleasant man eager to be helpful. Earning or not earning a tip did not affect his naturally pleasant personality. Lizzie said: "I'm afraid he does. I feel awkward without my shoes, my dresses, my makeup..."

"I'm sure he will be along shortly," said Harry diplomatically. They rose in a brass elevator cage. "You'll be in Room 302, Ma'am."

Lizzie said: "I am not expecting my husband today, but my brother and his wife will be checking sometime later. I've left instructions at the desk to notify me when they come."

"We'll keep an eye out, Mrs. Bernard. Don't you worry." On the third floor, Harry West led her out on a glassed-in balcony overlooking the central courtyard, then into a corridor above a stairwell, and immediately there was Room 302. Harry opened the door and showed her in. "Baths are at the end of the hall. Towels are in the closet. Please feel free at any time to ring me if you have any needs. There are shops below, including a druggist and a real estate office."

Lizzie said: "Thank you, Harry. There's one thing you could do for me."

Harry said: "Of course."

Lizzie pressed a healthy tip on him and said: "Bring me a large, empty bottle from the pharmacy, and a sponge please."

He looked amazed at the huge tip. "Certainly, but this is not necessary—a whole day's wages..."

Lizzie said: "Take it, please, with my good will. It does me good to know you are around and I can call on you. I suffer from the neuralgia, you know, and my doctor sent me to recuperate in this wonderful climate."

Harry West went down to the lobby and spoke with the Chief Clerk. A. S. Gomer said: "Have you tended to the peculiar woman everyone is talking about?"

Harry said: "I have. She tips magnificently and seems very nice."

Gomer said: "You don't think the fact she came alone, with no baggage, and looks like an actress, has any shady or immoral leanings to it?"

Harry shook his head. "Like I said, she seems to be a fine lady."

Gomer said: "These days, with the economy so bad, we'll take almost anybody. It appears she'll be paying day by day, which could be a bad sign in itself. " He shook his head, with a suspicious look.

Harry said: "She's running a tab, just so you know. I'm getting her a few items from the pharmacy. For her neuralgia."

A Pinkerton man approached the desk and addressed Gomer. He identified himself as Sam Dolbee as he displayed a badge. "You the manager?"

"Chief Clerk, sir. I double as manager sometimes."

Dolbee said: "Listen carefully. This must remain confidential. I am working on a situation for the management. You will talk to nobody about me, or anything I am working on, got that?"

"Yes!" Gomer's eyes widened. He gripped the desk with white knuckles.

"When I say confidential, I mean put big steel staples in your lips, or I will take you outside and do it to you myself."

A. S. Gomer said: "Yes sir! Whatever you need."

Dolbee said: "Let me see the guest register." He read the names and other information on the current day's page. After making some notes, he went to the hotel telephone and cranked the magneto. This put him in touch with an operator across the bay in San Diego, who in turn connected him with his boss Jeb Collins' office in the Pinkerton building.

Dolbee told Collins: "She signed in as Mrs. Lottie A. Bernard."

"Good. That checks with our information, so it's her."

"She gives her city of origin as Detroit."

"Good. I'll get the Detroit and Michigan people working on leads."

Dolbee added: "She expects her brother, a Dr. M. C. Anderson, and his wife Louisa to arrive any time."

"Hmmm. Sounds like accomplices."

"I agree."

"I get a feeling she's a phony. We'll have our Pinkerton offices check all the Bernards and Andersons in Greater Detroit, and any relatives they may have elsewhere in Michigan."

"Right." Dolbee rang off. He had another lead to check.

Dolbee knocked on a door on the third floor—Room 372. A sallow, middle-aged man opened the door. "Yes?"

"Mr. Joseph A. Jones?"

"Yes?"

"I'm with hotel security, doing a little routine investigation. Nothing to be alarmed about. Standard stuff. It's for the safety and well-being of our guests. I saw that you signed in right after a young lady—"

"Oh yes, the beautiful odd duck."

Dolbee whipped out his pad and said: "Now why do you call her that?"

Joseph A. Jones said: "By an amazing coincidence, I saw her on the train from Denver early this morning. She was having an argument with some cardsharp looking scoundrel."

Dolbee scribbled avidly. "Can you describe the man?"

"See here, I don't want to get involved in anything. I'm a businessman on a tight schedule. I have to be on a train out of state in two days, and I can't afford to get hung up in any local police work."

"Don't you worry, Mr. Jones. I'm not with the police. This is a private security matter. I'll say nothing about you to anyone. Just putting some information together. Now what can you tell me?" As Jones gave a good description of the man on the train, Dolbee was pleased—already, pieces were starting to fall into place.

In an atmosphere of dread, Lizzie slowly undressed. She stood naked by the night table. Her dress lay on the bed beside her. She felt a terrible unease about doing this, but she knew she had no choice but to trust Kate Morgan. Maybe John had just been having a bad day.

Her window overlooked the sunny intersection of Orange Avenue and two smaller side streets. Her room faced away from the ocean, east toward downtown Coronado, all three blocks of it. The room would get morning sun, but be in shade most of the day. She gazed out and forced herself to relax, to drift as best possible into a haze of positive thoughts.

Lizzie uncorked the bottle Harry West had brought. She poured it a third full of water from the wash jug on the bureau. She put the sponge into the ceramic bowl that came with the water jug. She opened the medicine box from the Hotel Brewster, and poured a fourth of the powder into the bottle. She corked the bottle and shook it well. Carefully opening it, she poured the resulting reddish, cloudy liquid into the sponge, in the ceramic wash bowl on the bureau, until the sponge had a wet spot in its center. She cringed a bit, alarmed by its blood-like color, as she pressed lightly to spread the liquid out. Then she poured a little more. She sat back in a chair and slowly and carefully pushed the sponge inside herself. It was a pessary, used since ancient Egyptian times for dosing the lower extremities of women. It could relieve constipation and menstrual cramps, or induce a deliberate miscarriage.

She also took quinine pills, which Kate said would help the process along, and chased the pills with a whiskey Harry West had brought at her request. There was also a small bottle of laudanum for pain—also known as tincture of opium, a powerful herbal mix of opium and alcohol—but she discovered someone had already taken most of it, and that was just another of many little knife pricks of betrayal.

When she was done, she dressed herself, and rested a while on the bed. She hoped that, at any minute, Harry would knock on the door and tell her that her brother and sister-in-law had arrived. But nobody came. The silence was oppressive, even ominous, as evening closed in. When it was dark outside, she went down to the front desk and spoke with Chief Clerk A. S. Gomer. "Hello—has my brother, Dr. Anderson, arrived or sent a message?"

"No, Mrs. Bernard. I am sorry, he has not."

"I—oh well, I am going to bed early tonight. It's been a long trip. I'm tired and want to go sight seeing tomorrow. I also have to figure out how to get my luggage from the depot, if my brother is delayed."

He looked at her, pityingly, looking a bit distrustful, and confused about these shadowy men in her life. "Good night, Mrs. Bernard. Sleep well. I will be on duty here tomorrow morning. Maybe I can call you a carriage then."

❧ ❦

Kate Morgan returned to the hotel room that afternoon. She lay curled up next to John Longfield, and fell into a deep slumber. Hours later, it seemed, she was startled awake by an unknown noise. The space by her side was cold. John was gone. She jumped out of bed and saw her purse lying open on the floor. "Oh, damn you!" What next? He had taken her money, but she knew where to find him. It reminded her of how they'd met—he'd been gambling with someone else's money. This situation was getting too complicated, too fast. She had never worked with anyone, besides her stint with Tom Morgan, and never this many people and this many loose ends. The situation threatened to come undone, and she didn't like it one bit. First, she must retrieve her incorrigible boyfriend. Why did men always seem to do things like this?

She got dressed and walked toward the Stingaree with all of its bedlam and mayhem. She heard distant gunshots and men whooping. Women shrilled suggestively, probably drunk. More gunshots, more laughter...

Kate came to the Yuma Building on Fifth Street, where she'd last seen Earp. His name was posted in a window, followed by the word *Capitalist*. In another window was a sign—*Gambling*. Kate entered.

She walked into a dark, noisy bar. The bartender told a lusty joke as he served up a brace of sudsy beers. Men laughed and talked—and ogled her.

Kate passed into a bigger room, whose door was marked *Cards*, and closed the door. The atmosphere was quiet and full of smoky concentration. Men puffing on cigars sat around tables poring over their cards. There he was—John Longfield, drinking, losing at poker, and red-faced. Before Kate could rescue him, John said: "You rigged that!" He threw his cards down and lurched to his feet, making fists.

Kate rushed toward him, but too late. Three plainclothes security men, their holstered guns in reach, rushed in and grabbed John by the scruff. One waved a cosh, but didn't use it on John's head. There was a scuffle and a sound of smacking flesh as the security men quickly led John out a back door marked *Office*.

Kate followed, and entered Wyatt Earp's office without knocking.

She froze at the door, with the handle in one hand. Nobody noticed her as she stood gaping. Wyatt Earp, still wearing his six-shooter, filled a pan with water at a small sink. He said: "No more liquor for our friend here."

The men pressed John down into a chair near the window. Earp poured water over a spluttering John's head, soaking him. "No more gambling here, bucko, ever again. You're a drunk and a sore loser. We look for guys like you and toss you on your ear."

John sputtered: "That guy was cheating."

"Yeah, maybe he does that now and then, but he makes money for the house. You're just an idiot who pisses his money away " Just then, Wyatt Earp spotted Kate. "Pardon me, Ma'am, my language—"

Kate said: "I've heard worse. I came to pick up my husband and take him home. If you see him in your saloons again, show him the door."

John looked at Kate with big red eyes and mussy hair as he sat dripping. At Earp's signal, the security men backed away. Kate said to John: "You go home right now and I'll see you there. Don't you dare go left or right, but straight to our room and wait there for me." She said to Earp: "Can I bend your ear a moment?"

Earp waved his men out, and they accompanied John out the door.

Earp and Kate were alone. Kate said: "You were watching the Brewster the other day. I was out getting my hair done and saw you."

Wyatt Earp said: "There is almost nothing around the New City that I don't learn about. Why is this of any importance to you?"

Kate said: "We all have our reasons, Mr. Earp. I have a bit of information for you. By the way, I'm surprised and glad to meet the famous lawman. I had no idea it was you."

He seemed good-natured enough, though shrewd and suspicious. "So what can I help you with?"

Kate said: "Well, to begin with, I thought you'd like to know Pinkerton has a tail on you."

He frowned. "How would you know? Are you with Pinkerton?"

"No, I came looking for my husband." She thought quickly and made up a fib. "I saw you outside the Brewster, and the man following you. I was having my hair done, and saw my good-for-nothing husband go by. As I was looking for Doug, I saw the man following you. He went into the Pinkerton building."

Wyatt Earp said: "I have news for you. Now that you came here, the same people will start tailing you. I know about them."

"What do you know about them?"

"Nothing to tell," he lied, and they both knew it. He eyeballed her strangely, though his smile never faded. Just a refocusing of light, in those sharp-as-glass eyes, by the instincts of an experienced lawman.

"So now you got yourself into the game. Where are you staying, anyway?"

"Coronado," Kate lied. "Why should I be concerned, Mr. Earp?"

Wyatt Earp relented and said: "I play my cards close to the chest. Something big is going on in town. The cops and the Pinkertons always come to me. This is one of those times, but I have no idea what that would be. Are you involved in whatever it is?" He regarded her closely.

Kate slipped into her most innocent persona. "Not at all. Just trying to stay out of trouble, collect my drunken husband, and get him home before he gets into trouble. Thanks for not roughing him up too much."

Wyatt Earp said: "I don't like roughing men up, Mrs.—"

"Katie Lomax. "

"And what do you do, Mrs. Lomax?"

"I am a domestic servant in rich people's homes. My husband was a book binder, but he recently lost his job."

Wyatt Earp had a twinkle in his eyes: "Not a book maker, eh?"

"You are a great man, and funny! So it's nothing my husband got himself involved in then?"

"Your husband, involved in something so big that it's got a whole mess of Pinkertons running around town?" Wyatt Earp laughed at the thought. "Nahhh. We are small fry in Mr. Spreckels' grand schemes, whatever those may be."

"Oh, the rich guy," Kate said.

"I think it's about him, because the Hotel del Coronado has come up in conversation, and he owns it. I'm not one to serve any rich man. I'm out to protect my own interests. I don't owe a thing to any man. I have four gambling establishments and I partner on some fine racing horses at Del Mar. What I'm afraid of is Mr. Spreckels is going to clean up the Stingaree, now that he owns most of San Diego and all of Coronado, and those temperance people hate gambling as much as they hate drink. So I keep an eye out for anything that affects me."

The door opened, and the beautiful former actress Josephine Marcus entered, age 31, carrying a basket of wash. Despite her dowdy clothes, torn apron, and a kerchief around her dark hair, she looked exotic and stunning, as in lithos Kate had seen in gossipy magazines. Josie held a large wicker basket full of laundry in both hands. "I'm sorry to interrupt, folks. Wyatt, love, do you have anything for this basket? Ah Wong is taking a load to the laundry."

Wyatt Earp said to his wife: "No, love, thanks." He told Kate: "Mrs. Lomax, meet my wife, Josie Marcus. Josie, Mrs. Lomax." Then he told Josie: "We were just helping her husband with a problem."

Josie Earp said: "From the look of that floor, you gave him a bath. Did he have fleas?"

"You are so lovely and famous. I've read about you." She'd seen a famous glamour shot of Josie, wrapped in mystery, and titillating..

Josie Marcus said: "Those days are long behind me."

Kate said: "I have a friend who would love to meet you—but she's not in town just now." She was thinking of Lizzie, who loved theater.

Josie Marcus said: "I still get letters from admirers from my Tombstone days. Excuse me. I have to hurry! Nice meeting you!" She sidled out the door, turning to maneuver the large laundry basket. To Kate, the actress looked perfectly happy in her new role as housewife.

Earp said: "Good luck, Mrs. Lomax. Keep your eye on Mr. Lomax so he stays out of trouble."

"Thank you, Mr. Earp. It has been a lot of fun meeting you and your lovely wife." Kate's spine crawled as she left. She felt his eyes boring into her back.

Lizzie came down to the desk and got the chief clerk's attention. "Good morning, Mr. Gomer. Any word from my brother?"

"Nothing yet, Mrs. Bernard, I am sorry."

"There's also my other problem. My brother ran off with the claim tickets for my luggage up north the other day. I have no clothes, no shoes, no jewelry to wear. I'll have to cross the bay to speak with someone at the baggage terminal."

"I wish I could help you there. I understand they are sticklers for the rules. Maybe you should wait until your brother arrives with the tickets so you don't waste a trip."

She sighed deeply. "I'll check with you again to see if Dr. Anderson has arrived. I'll have something to eat, and then go for a walk."

"Relaxation—that's the key with the neuralgia. We see a lot of it here at the resort. Enjoy your day, Mrs. Bernard."

Lizzie ate a leisurely breakfast in the Coronet dining area near the main lobby. She had coffee, English muffin, eggs scrambled, bacon, tomatoes, and cereal with cream. As much as she enjoyed it, she was beginning to feel an aching heaviness in her lower torso, which told her the medicine was beginning to take effect. Being pregnant already changed much in one's body, but this was all the more strange and different. It affected how she sat, how she walked, or even bent forward to grab the table salt.

After lunch, Lizzie walked along the beach. The sun streamed down on her, and she closed her eyes and looked up at it as if it were a medicinal shower.

She came to Star Stables, and saw a frisky stallion. Walking closer, she asked a groom about it, and he directed her to a cashier's office. She rented the horse, had it saddled, and climbed aboard. No sooner was she astride the saddle, than the horse bucked and would not do her bidding. For a moment, she was afraid to fall off backwards and get kicked. As she cried out, along came teenage stable-hand Charlie Stevens. He took the animal firmly in hand. "They haven't gelded him yet," he apologized. "They should not have given you this one."

Lizzie said: "Please help me. I want to get off." He held the reins in one hand, and offered his other hand. "Thank you, Charlie," she said as she dismounted. "Whew!"

"Are you visiting from out of town?"

"I'm staying at the resort for my neuralgia," Lizzie said: "Do you have a carriage? And someone to drive it?"

Charlie grinned. "That would be me, Ma'am, if you will permit me. I will gladly take you on a tour of the area." At her bidding, he harnessed the wayward horse to a carriage. It submitted meekly, glad to be under firm hand. Lizzie sat in the carriage while Charlie trotted them out for a tour of Coronado. As he would later tell a newspaper reporter, on that day Lizzie looked robust and in the pink of health despite the medicines she was already taking.

Back in her room that evening, Lizzie took another dose of pills, and redid her pessary. Before going to bed, she wandered down into the lobby, which sported large chandeliers lit by electric power. She stopped to ask the front desk clerks about her brother, but there was still no word. She held her stomach in discomfort as she rode the elevator out of sight.

As was her frequent habit, in the morning Lizzie stopped at the front desk. It was becoming like the refrain in a song. Lizzie said: "Has Dr. Anderson sent any word for me yet?"

As always, the clerks shook their heads solemnly.

Lizzie went for a walk along the beach. She still wore the clothes she had come with, and they were starting to look shabby. Elegant women carrying parasols turned to stare at her with haughty, withering glances. She walked to the water's edge and looked south at a distant ship. How strange and disembodied she felt! How much like a dream all this was! She watched a seagull fly past.

Nearby stood a charming looking man in his 30s, with a mustache. He wore dark trousers and a white shirt open at the neck, with no collar or tie. He was barefoot, and struck her as funny because his feet looked pink and uncomfortable. Lizzie laughed as she picked up a pebble and threw it out over the water. The pebble skipped several times before vanishing.

The man said: "Bravo! Five skips."

Lizzie said: "Oh, hi," in an easy, familiar way, as if they knew each other.

He sauntered closer. He seemed harmless and friendly at the first glance.

"Are you laughing at me?"

"Your feet. They look as if they are squinting at the sunlight. They wish they were back in their shoes.

He laughed. Looking down, he wiggled his toes. "You're right." He and she both laughed. Lizzie felt good to have something to laugh about, and someone to laugh with. He said: "Are you here on holiday?"

Lizzie said: "I'm here to recover from a bout of the neuralgia. The doctor says I am the worrying type, and he sent me here to rest."

He said: "Me too. I live in Chicago but I'm thinking of moving here with my family. I came to explore the Theosophical Society."

Lizzie said: "What's that?" She skipped more pebbles as they spoke.

He pointed west to the long, misty pile of Point Loma and Cabrillo Point sticking out darkly into the sea. "They are building their society up there on the point. I have a nervous ailment that I'm told this climate and their spiritualist theories may help. My name is Frank." He stuck out his hand. "And you are—?"

"My name is Lottie. I am staying here at the hotel." She was going to add *with my husband and my brother and his wife*, but what was the point in fibbing? It was beginning to dawn on her that neither John nor Kate had any intention of contacting her until the game was over. She must stay here and soldier on, waiting for word, and if no word came, it meant Spreckels wasn't paying up. Then she would take the last of her medicines and collapse in a lake of blood in the middle of his hotel lobby. And they would either save her, or she would die, and she no longer entirely cared which solution it was. Either way, she would be freed of the terrible burdens she had borne. And she felt terrible at the suffering this would impose on the life growing within her. It would all be over in a few days, one way or another.

The great epiphany came to her as she stood like a child, skipping pebbles on the sea, and talking with this pleasant, innocent man who reminded her suddenly what it was like to speak with a decent human being once again. She almost told him her real name, but realized maybe she wasn't really herself anymore. All of this came to her in a sudden flash of insight. The sun shone, the sea smelled fresh, the wind was frisky like that puppy she saw playing with children in the tide nearby, and she felt lightened. She realized what must now happen, what she must do—only, not now; tomorrow. It could be put off in honor of this beautiful day and her enjoyment of it. "So what do you do, Frank?"

"Why—I am a professional failure, a fool, and a burden to my wife."

Lizzie said: "You sound a lot like me, except I have no spouse. I have nobody. I am all alone in the world." She thought again of the child she had once given up, and the changes taking place in her body. She thought about spiritualism, of which she had heard, and looked southeast at the sun hanging reddish-yellow over distant water. She understood now. Beauty, like happiness, could be seen but not touched, like that light rippling over water, ephemeral as light and shadow.

The way the sea washed gently up on the earth, pulled by the moon, and washed out in its rhythms twice daily, Lizzie herself felt like the earth and the sea, containing but not owning life or beauty. She had nothing to do in this moment but let nature show its full beauty, with Lizzie and the great hotel and the beautiful sea and this wonderful man and all these people parts of that greater, unified whole as the wonderful moments flickered by, *the golden atoms of the day* as she'd read once in a romantic poem.

In giving up control, or the illusion of control, she gained total power. And what was power? She held up her hand, opening it, as if power was just wind that blew between her fingers. Everything seemed so clear now, if slightly out of phase due to the medicines, and maybe she needed to eat something. But she felt content.

"You poor young lady."

Lizzie smiled comfortably. "So what does a professional failure do?"

Frank said: "I've tried everything from acting to writing, from raising fancy poultry to running a theater. My chickens died, the theater failed, my scripts burned, and my health collapsed." Lizzie held her hand over her mouth. They laughed again together. Soon they were both howling with laughter and slapping each other on the back. It was all in the moment. People looked at them, turning from conversations to crane their necks and see what the laughter was, and the world seemed to be smiling with the slightly shabby, very pretty girl who seemed so free, and the shoeless man. Finally, Lizzie and he caught their breath. They strolled along the beach.

Frank said: "It does a man good to laugh at himself. And to be laughed at by a beautiful woman."

"I wasn't laughing at you. I was laughing at your story. It all seems to blend so well—the chickens, the burning pages, the theater..."

"And you, Lottie? What do you do?"

"I am a rain cloud."

"What?"

"I cry very easily, so sad have I lately been. But you don't want to hear of my troubles, nor would I want to share them with anyone."

Frank said: "You are a very smart young lady. That was a clever conceit about the tears and the rain cloud."

"That's very sweet of you to say. I wonder, Frank, if people all around the world said pleasant things to each other, and made each other laugh, if it would be a cure for neuralgia and all of humanity's ills."

"I bet it would work. Well, I am trying to think of a children's book to write. I have some ideas."

Lizzie said: "Like what?"

"I lived in the Dakota Territory not long ago, and it was amazing to see how a tornado could sweep up people and animals and wagons and fly them through the air and then set them down a mile away. Sometimes in smithereens, sometimes unscathed. It might be a fun adventure to write a story about some people who are animals, and animals who are people, that get swept away to an imaginary land in the ozone, and have adventures. A little bit like Alice in Wonderland. I could call it Thunderland. Make a good theater play also."

Lizzie said: "I love theater. Did you meet any famous actresses during your theater years?"

"Why yes—quite a few. Their fame and fortune didn't rub off on me."

"Now Frank. Talk about a rain cloud. You seem to always make such a misery of yourself. Be positive."

"I'm sorry. Do I do that? Thanks for pointing that out to me."

"I believe that if you force yourself to smile, you will believe you are happy. Of course that's easy for an old rain cloud to say."

Frank said: "You are a very wise old rain cloud."

"Belatedly."

"What troubles you so, Lottie? I sense that, under all that sunshine and beauty, you carry a heavy stone on your heart."

"You're right, Frank. I've made some poor decisions, and now I have to carry the rocks."

"And you don't want to unburden yourself of them? We've scarcely met, but I already think of you as a dear friend."

Lizzie said: "No, it's just as well that I keep my mistakes to myself. But I do appreciate your kind companionship. You are a married man, and nothing untoward must pass between us."

"Oh heavens, my intentions are pure."

"I sense that about you. A woman would see through me instantly, but a man has a certain innocence. And I think I am really a very nice girl, who has trusted other people too much. Enough of that. It sounds like you want to write a children's story."

Frank said: "I think that's what it wants to be."

"Tell me a bit more about your ideas. It makes me feel so light and happy to forget my own troubles."

So L. Frank Baum proceeded to tell her the earliest inklings he had of what would become a great classic, *The Wonderful Wizard of Oz*, to be published in 1900, and on whose sequels he would work at the Hotel del Coronado. But that lay in the future, when all the footsteps of this day, and many of the people who made them, would be long washed away by the tide.

While Lizzie and Frank chatted on the beach, Pinkerton detective Sam Dolbee was going through Lizzie's belongings in her room. He had obtained a key from A. S. Gomer, and now looked like a gray shadow, bent over the Detroit woman's meager belongings.

In a dim, shadowy light, he saw the medicine box on the table. He ran his fingertip over her medicine vial, delicately, as if he were afraid the dully gleaming glass would cut him. The liquid inside looked a muddy red color, like congealing blood. The white label, with its red border lines, was marked in blue ink using a dipping pen in a blocky penmanship whose author could be male or female. A note in plainer pen lay near the vial. The note read: *If the pain gets too bad, see the doctor*. It was signed simply *Druggist*. No official markings like *Rx*. He left everything exactly as he found it, barely brushing his fingertip over surfaces as he gazed with critical, inquisitive eyes.

His gaze stabbed around the room, with its three windows facing

Orange Avenue. The room had a fireplace, bed, table, chair, and a bureau whose drawers were all empty—nothing else. He found nothing under the bureau. He pawed through her satchel. He ran his hands under the mattress, but found nothing. He ran his fingers over the window and door frames, finding nothing but dust. If she had the love letters of which she had written in her blackmail note to Spreckels, they were well hidden. He could find no sign of them, and time was running out. She must not find him in her room. It was imperative that she (and any possible accomplices) be watched without knowing they were under observation. That would make it easier to catch any slip-ups she (or they) made.

Just before he left the room, tiptoeing out as quietly as he had entered, and leaving no sign of his presence, he did find several faded hankies embroidered with a name that was hard to make out—Lizzie Anderson. He made a note of the name. He would telephone his superior Jeb Collins, in San Diego, and tell him to quickly start a search around Detroit for anyone named Anderson or Lizzie Anderson, and all the variants on that name and their relatives in other cities in Michigan. Detroit was the city she gave on the hotel's register as her origin. Like so many other particulars of the case, the local police and the coroner would learn nothing from him. They did not even know the two Pinkerton Special Agents were on the case. The client they served was not the truth, nor the better good of humanity, but John Spreckels.

Frank and Lizzie sauntered along the beach, chatting and laughing at little jokes. Frank said: "It's getting late, and I have to get back to Point Loma for dinner with the Theosophists." He pointed to the peninsula sticking out into the ocean to their west, framing the harbor entrance.

Lizzie said: "You don't know how much it's helped me to have your company this afternoon."

"I must tell you the same, since I'm alone here on business. You are so sad, Lottie. Despite your beauty and your many smiles, your eyes look haunted. Won't you unburden yourself? I'm a good listener."

"It's best I don't, Frank. It's just as well. Humor me. "

"Is it some illness far worse than your neuralgia?"

"Now that you say it, it's love."

"That can be a terrible sickness."

"When you've been betrayed and abandoned, yes. Not only by your *beau*, but by your friends."

Frank looked at his watch as it grew darker. "I have to run, much as it pains me. Will you be here tomorrow?"

Lizzie extended a hand and smiled sadly. "I can't see you, Frank. Not that I fear that you plan to mash me or anything." They both laughed. "I just think it's best that I spend the day resting and reading."

They shook hands and parted, going their separate ways.

Alone in her room, Lizzie took more medicine. She settled on her bed to read, and soon fell asleep clutching her stomach as the pain grew worse.

On Sunday morning, Lizzie awoke with stabbing pains. With a drawn-out, low wail moan, she staggered to the table and swallowed more pills. She chased them with water. Sitting down hard, she rang for bellman Harry West.

Harry arrived quickly at the open door. "How are you today, Mrs. Bernard. Oh, you don't look so well."

"I don't feel well." She handed him a dollar. "Can you bring me a cocktail and some wine?"

He took the money reluctantly. "It's a bit early in the day, isn't it?"

"I need something. And I plan to take a bath and wash my clothes. I still have not gotten my baggage checks, nor have I heard from my brother and his wife. Will you draw hot water for me?"

"Whatever you say. But do you think it's a good idea, getting yourself wet, and your hair wet too—it might make your illness worse."

"I think a bath will be relaxing, and I have to wash my clothes. I have never before, in my entire life, had to wear the same clothes three days in a row. "

"I'll be back with some towels in a little while. I'll heat water and run down to get your drinks."

A while later, Lizzie sat alone in the steamy bath room, washing her clothes while sipping wine. The door was locked, and nobody knocked to bother her. Lizzie wrung out her skirt, her blouse, and her undies and stockings, and hung them up on a clothes line the hotel had strung along one tiled wall for the benefit and comfort of female guests.

It took effort to climb into the tub, holding her drink. The warmth wrapped around her aching lower torso, and comforted her achy thighs. She rested and soaked in the tub. The wine brought a blush to her cheeks, and she felt drowsy.

She grew light-headed. The glass started to slip from her hand, and she was barely able to lean over and put it on the floor. The glass keeled over, without breaking, and made a blood-colored puddle on the floor's tiny, patterned white tiles. She spit up something reddish-purple, maybe a mix of blood and wine. She wasn't sure. Her body felt paralyzed, and for a moment it seemed a dark force was pulling her under. It felt like quicksand working on her. Consciousness ebbed and returned in waves like the tides out at the beach. This dark sea, however, felt like a dozen arms, like a painting she had seen in a magazine, of nightmarish evil water nymphs, pulling her down to a watery death. Recalling her epiphany on the beach, she struggled inwardly. *Please. It's not time yet. I'm not ready today.* Darkness rose up, and next thing she knew, she wasn't breathing—her face was in the water.

She lifted her head like a drowning person, cried out, and clutched the side of the bath. The water in the tub sloshed hard and noisily around her from the panicked motion. She clung to the tub with her head and hair hanging down the outside. The floor was covered with water. She retched, and a string of blood-red vomit and undigested food fell to the tiles.

She half climbed, half fell from the tub. Slipping on the wet floor, she wrapped herself in a heavy white robe Harry had provided. She staggered out of the bathroom, down the hall, toward her room. She braced herself against the wall with one arm, while the other flailed and she half stumbled several times on rubbery knees. Harry happened to be passing by (or hovering concernedly about) and he helped her to the room. His face portrayed shock.

In her room, Lizzie sat gravely ill on the chair while Harry toweled her hair dry. "Thank you, Harry."

Harry said: "You're far more ill than you said."

"It's just a bad case of neuralgia."

"I'll clean up the bath room and get your clothing. Don't you worry."

"It's good of you to care so much. Can you bring me some hot broth?"

L izzie was alone, and felt a bit better, after eating the bouillon Harry brought her, along with bits of buttered French bread and black coffee. Wearing a fresh hotel bathrobe, she sat at the table. She chewed idly on a pencil and played with some scraps of paper. On one scrap she doodled pictures, and wrote: *Frank Frank Frank Frank*—pining for his company. As she remembered the pleasant man she'd met on the beach, she said out loud: "Frank Frank Frank Frank—oh, if only my John were more a man like you. Everything would be so totally different."

The pain ebbed and flowed. She went down to see the legitimate pharmacist in the basement shops to buy a quantity of laudanum. He sold her a bottle with a red skull and crossbones symbol of terrible danger on it. He asked her about her pain, and urged her to see a doctor. She had no intention of doing so.

Back in the room she took a spoonful, and welcomed the numbness it brought. She thought of this whole mess that Kate had convinced her to be involved in. She had no desire to hurt John Spreckels, who had done her no harm. She scribbled: *I hardly know that man—I have only heard of him.* To Kate, wherever she might be, she said: "I thought I could trust you, and you never showed up. You and John both. And I don't have the evil in me to harm this great and powerful man I don't even know." She started to rise, but fell from the chair. On her hands and knees, she crawled to the closet. In the shadows, she lifted a wooden floor board. She pulled out the love letters Kate had given her. She was to give these to a messenger who would come in exchange for the money that would be wired to a bank. She would do the right thing now, and burn these things. But she felt too weak. She left the letters strewn on the wooden closet floor, and pushed the closet door shut. She half crept, half walked and fell, to the bed. There, wracked by spasms of pain, Lizzie held her stomach and lay in a fetal position.

A while later, she woke when Harry West brought her a bowl of oatmeal and some wine. She sat up and felt happy to see him and the food. "I thought you might like these. You look a little better, Mrs. Bernard."

"Thank you, Harry. What would I do without you?" Slowly, she walked to the table, sat on the chair, and took the spoon he handed her. The oatmeal had milk and brown sugar in it, and some sliced apples. "Oh, this is divine. Thank you."

Harry West said: "Anything else before I leave for home?"

Lizzie said: "Thanks, Harry. Run along to your wife and children. Come see me tomorrow."

"I will." He gave her shoulder a light squeeze, in answer to her plaintive tone. After he left, she ate, and then sipped the wine. She gathered the letters for now, and put them back in their hiding place. She amused herself, writing imaginary invitations to Lottie Bernard from famous actresses. Lizzie read out loud as she wrote: "Miss Louise Leslie Carter, star of the stage and theater, wishes to invite you to a pleasant stay at the famous Hotel del Coronado." She paused with dreamy smile and wrote as she said: "Miss Lillian Russell requests the honor of your company on a visit to the Hotel del Coronado." She paused, then continued: "Mr. Denman Thompson, author of the famous play 'The Old Homestead'…"

Lizzie paused at a lack for words. She had a coughing spell and crawled to the bed, debilitated. Light burned low in the fireplace as night wrapped itself around her.

In the gray dawn light on Monday, Lizzie lay sleeping on her bed. Daylight was just beginning to penetrate the darkness, driving night away. Outside, it was a cold and drizzly day. A great sea storm was coming, and the atmosphere was charged with strange electricities as if sensing the storm raging inside her. Someone knocked on the door.

Lizzie slept on.

A rough hand rattled the door handle—not a hand intending kindness.

Still Lizzie slept.

A key turned in the lock. It was a sharp, slicing sound, like someone cutting with a knife. The man whose hands were on the door paused. The door opened, and Lizzie started up from her sleep. She could not reach her glasses. Her vision was blurry, and she couldn't move, as a man intruded in the room and stood by the bed. He smelled cold and smoky, like tobacco and cheap soap. She tried to sit up, but he roughly shoved her back. The intruder said: "We know you are here under an alias."

Lizzie swallowed hard, could not speak. She squinted at his dark, blurry outline. He said: "Who are your accomplices? We know you are working with a man and a woman."

Lizzie reached for a water glass. It fell and shattered.

He was relentless, in a cold tone as even and sharp as a knife blade. "The game is over, Lizzie. Yes, we know your name. You can sign this paper—" She heard a sheet of paper rattle. "—And we will pay you something to leave town. What do you say? It's your only hope. I won't be back to ask you again."

Lizzie tried to nod, but only managed a shake of her head that he took for a no.

"Very well then. I'll give you twenty-four hours. If you have not changed your mind by then, we will arrest you. Nobody will pay you the blackmail money, and we won't allow you to ruin our client's good name. Trust me, we have dealt with vermin like you many times, and the outcome is always terrible for your kind. Think about sitting in a cold, smelly, dirty prison cell for the rest of your life. That's the only future in store for you." The intruder made a blurry, hazy exit, sort of jerky, like a reflection in a rain puddle that kept coming apart in slices, and then slid biliously back together, only to balloon and break apart again. Lizzie coughed up watery blood and yellowish bile as she fell back into unconsciousness.

Kate Morgan and John Longfield sat together talking in their hotel room. They were affectionate with one other, but the atmosphere was tense. Kate said: "It's Monday. We were going to give it five days. Time's up tomorrow. I have a crawling sensation."

John said: "You want to get Lizzie and pull her out? Can you imagine if something went wrong, and she told the coppers about us?"

Kate said: "You're right. Let's not waste another minute. I don't relish ending up in prison for many years. Let's go across to Coronado and get her out. We'll take her to a doctor, and she can have her miscarriage. Then at least your problem is solved. I will find another day to scalp Mr. Spreckels, or someone like him." She thought about it. "On the other hand, Johnny, you stay here, out of sight. I'll go out and run some errands, and get a message to her. It's best if we stay as low as possible."

"You always know best," John said.

"I'll be back after dark," Kate said. She put on her hat and shawl, and started for the door. She needed a walk, and some time to think. What was the best way to end this without leaving a trail for the police? She must be very careful. At least she would not have clumsy John dashing her plans. And she really could not leave Lizzie behind. "Stay here," she admonished him, and let herself out. Before she left, she instructed him: "I'm going to send a note across, telling her to meet me and you secretly after midnight on the back steps. It will be rainy. We can leave together without being seen. You lay low here, and don't do anything without me. Got that?"

"I got it, darling. You can rely on me."

Kate closed the door and hurried off down the corridor.

John pulled a bag full of beer bottles out from under the bed. He lit a cigar, gave a sigh of satisfaction, and opened the first bottle.

The damp, gray air that met Kate Morgan was far from the balmy, sunny normal climate of San Diego. It was a wall of gray maritime moisture, like a thick fog blanketing everything. In the distance reared the black clouds of a terrible sea storm that was about to hit that night. People said it was expected to be a storm of the century.

L izzie lay in her room at the Hotel del Coronado, suffering intensely. Gray light filtered into the room from the heavy marine layer outside. The room was chilly, and the little fireplace was full of cold ash. Her medications were strewn on the table, along with the scraps of paper and her hankies. Her satchel hung on a hook behind the door.

She heard Harry West outside, even before he knocked. Lizzie could not force herself to answer, nor stir. Harry used his pass key to let himself in. "Mrs. Bernard—are you okay?"

Lizzie turned weakly, and whispered. "Thank God, Harry. Bring me something hot."

Harry ran from the room. A while later, he returned with a tray of hot steaming tea and cereal with milk. "You have to eat. Can you sit up?"

Lizzie nodded and sat up. As she ate from the tray he placed on her lap, she asked: "Do you have some matches?"

He fumbled in his pockets. "Yeah, I think I have a few in my pocket. Will this do?" He showed her three or four wooden matches.

"Those will do." She nodded and took them.

Someone knocked on the door. She said "Enter," fearing that terrible man and his threats was returning.

Chief Clerk Gomer came in, looking serious. "Good morning, Mrs. Bernard. Please pardon my intrusion. It's freezing in here." He shuddered. "Shall I have Harry light your fire for you?"

Lizzie said: "No..."

"Mrs. Bernard, Harry has told me how ill you are. This is nothing to fool around with. I suggest calling the house physician."

Lizzie panicked at the idea of a doctor figuring out what she was doing to herself, so she fibbed. "No, there is no use. I am terminally ill with stomach cancer. I was hoping my brother would come, but he seems to be delayed. I am dying, Mr. Gomer, and wish to be left alone."

A. S. Gomer looked shocked. "Mrs. Bernard, if there is anything—."

Lizzie said: "There is nothing. I am told I only have days to live." It sounded silly even to her own ears. And yet—

Gomer told Harry: "Light a fire. Don't charge her for the service." To Lizzie he said: "Mrs. Bernard, I must ask if you will be able to pay the credit charges you have accumulated. They amount to more than twenty dollars by now."

Lizzie nodded. "Yes, there is money on account for me at the bank in Washington, Iowa. You have only to telegraph them, and they will forward a Western Union wire draft."

"Thank you," Gomer said, and left.

Harry meanwhile started a little fire, using scraps of paper and kindling in a basket beside the fireplace. He stirred the fire with the poker that stood in a corner. "This will warm you up a bit."

"Thanks, Harry."

Alone in the room, Lizzie lay sleeping.

She woke to pull a chamber pot from under the bed to retch in it. She fell back asleep, with her hand dangling off the bed and her fingers loosely holding the handle of the soiled white ceramic pot.

As the morning wore on, she slowly rose and went to the closet. She gathered up the love notes of Spreckels and Charlotte Barnard. She fanned the coals to get the fire going solidly. Effortfully, she started tearing the letters up one by one and fed them to the fire. The room grew warmer and brighter. Harry stopped by to check on her, and saw her burning the documents, as he would soon testify.

Kate Morgan was on her way down to the ferry landing. As she came down D Street, she approached the California Southern Railway's train station. She stopped in at the telegraph office, as she did every day, to see if there was anything for Charlotte Barnard. She would simply walk by the postal boxes, and see if there was a slip of paper behind the little glass window. She knew the box was being watched, and would not actually go near it. Her plan, if she saw something inside, was to telegraph her old school friend Allen in Iowa and see if Spreckels had wired the money, as they had arranged last month. By now, she realized the hopes of that were scant to none. The box was empty. She borrowed some writing materials at a table set aside for customers, and wrote a note for Lizzie, pretending it was from John: *Lizzie, the game is up. I will come by this evening to get you. Look for me, and if all else fails, meet me on the back stairs outside after midnight. I love you always—John L.*.

Her intention was to send John to fetch her under cover of night, and let him take the risk of being caught.

As she sealed the envelope and tucked it in her pocket, and started to exit the telegraph office, she almost had a heart attack.

There, tacked to the wooden door, was a picture of her husband, Tom Morgan. He looked exactly as he had when she last saw him—the thick head, the receding dark hair, the pleasant face with slightly crazy eyes. Underneath the photograph was a note: *Kate, if you read this, contact me at the Hotel Brewster. I have much to tell you. Love you forever, Tom*.

Shaken, she looked left and right and hurried out into the street. What a damned complication! She no longer loved Tom, nor did she believe he had changed. It would be as before—lovey dovey one day, then drinking and beatings the next. She could never forgive him for kicking her down the stairs, killing their unborn child, and leaving her barren. Reviewing that incident alone in her thoughts, she firmly and absolutely made up her mind. She would never go back to him. But dammit—he was the last thing she needed right now. What luck, to spot his note. Now at least he would not surprise her if he spotted her on the street of this small town. She must be extra vigilant. Pulling the brim of her black straw hat low, she hurried across the street to a lunch counter, and ordered a little beer to sip while she deliberated what to do next. In this dim gray light, people moved about like hazy shadows. Lights burned, and animals slunk away seeking shelter. The barometric pressure was dropping, and a chill drizzle hung in the air along with a sour scent of wood smoke. The train that pulled out of the station looked like a long, dark smoke-wraith threaded with rows of blurry yellow lanterns. Its hard chuffing and the slam of its gear shafts made steel scream on steel. It was almost as if the train were struggling to escape, which mirrored the cold panic Kate Morgan felt. Her collapsing plans enclosed her like a trapped animal in a cage. Kate's main thought now was to get Lizzie out of there, and herself and John and Lizzie out of San Diego. She would get Lizzie to a doctor, and make her promise never to tell what she had been involved in—yes, that was it, Lizzie and John would be glad to get out of San Diego safe and secure, with no police troubles. Spreckels would most likely keep the matter secret. And Kate had to figure out how to escape back into the vastness of the continental United States, maybe lie low for a year or two, work as a domestic, until all this blew over. That was her state of mind as she finished her beer, and walked down to the ferry. She asked around until she found a reputable looking young man and woman headed for the Hotel del Coronado. She asked them if they would deliver her note, which was addressed to Mrs. Lottie A. Bernard, directly to her room, which Kate by now had learned was Number 302 on the third floor. The young couple were very nice, realizing the importance that Kate put on it, and promised to slide it directly under Lizzie's door.

Kate watched the ferry—a large gray ship capable of carrying horses and buggies in addition to passengers—leave the dock on its fifteen-minute steam-powered journey across roughly a quarter mile of San Diego Bay, from the landing near G Street to the foot of Orange Avenue in Coronado.

℞ ℟

Tom Morgan walked the streets of San Diego, looking for his wife. Passion burned in his chest and gorge as he thought of her in bed with him. Here he was, close to her at last, in this small city. He had sometimes wept with despair and remorse at losing her because of his faults. At other times, he could just as easily weep with rage at what she had done to him, abandoning him, and she being his lawfully wedded wife! They had been two souls together, with the world against them, and now they would be together again, by whatever it took to make it happen.

He'd take a few drinks to calm himself, and try to think constructively. He kept pretty much sober except for a bracing whiskey or two at times like this. The best idea, he thought, had been the pictures—having his photo taken and posting copies in prominent spots around town. That should get her attention. Meanwhile, he spent every waking hour walking around looking for her.

Tom's path soon took him, in a day or so, to the Stingaree. There, he visited Wyatt Earp's dining and gambling establishments and ate a nice steak dinner with cold beer. Lighting a fresh cigar, he took a walk through the card rooms, but had no interest in gambling just now. His mind was on Kate.

In this hopeful, virtuous frame of mind, he met the great lawman and his beautiful actress wife. He introduced himself simply as Tom, a visitor from Nebraska, and Earp was very cordial. Tom had visited some of Earp's former stomping grounds like Dodge City, Kansas, and Tombstone, Arizona. Earp put a hand on his shoulder and invited him to the bar for a whisky, which Tom gladly accepted. "So what brings you to town?" Wyatt asked by way of conversation, while the bartender set their shot glasses before them.

"On me," Wyatt said. He and Tom clinked glasses and downed the drinks.

"Thank you, Sir," said Tom. Tom knew the man was studying him attentively behind that easy-going front and that imposing mustachio. No matter—whatever Earp hoped to learn about him, he hoped to learn what he could. They set their glasses aside. Tom said: "I've come to San Diego in search of my poor wife." He offered Wyatt a sanitized tale about how they had an argument a few years ago, and she had some other troubles, and left him. Now he had had time to think over his sins, and regret the times he spoke sharply to her, and wished to find her and get before her on his knees and beg her to come back.

"What does she look like?" Wyatt asked innocently. Tom, just as innocently, described Kate while ordering a second round on himself. Wyatt lifted his drink and froze. "Why, that describes a Mrs....." He downed his drink. "Now what was her name?"

Tom shot his down and set his glass aside, feeling a hot tingle both from the whisky and from Wyatt's frowning effort to recall a woman he had recently met.

"There was a woman who said her name was Claire something. She came to get her drunken idiot husband. That wouldn't be her. Naw."

"I'm clutching at straws," Tom said. "Any idea where they're staying?"

"Oh, some hotel downtown. Now wait a moment. It seems to me she mentioned something about Coronado at one point."

"The island across the bay?" Tom asked.

"I remember her name now. It was Claire Lomax, and she lied to me. She wasn't staying in Coronado."

"A lie, eh? That sounds more like my Katie already."

"For reasons of my own, I did some leg work. I learned she and that man are staying at a hotel near India and Date. I'll give you directions."

Tom thanked him and bought another round. Wyatt Earp explained about the wonderful resort that Elisha Babcock and Hampton Story had built during the boom years. The two men had developed Coronado from a forlorn wilderness full of jack rabbits into an upscale city that was incorporated in 1891. Spreckels had bought them out, like so much else. Wyatt worried that Spreckels and the do-gooders were going to clean up San Diego, get rid of the Stingaree, and drive out all of Wyatt's business.

Tom left the saloon elatedly, and fortified with a few drinks. Thinking of the man she was with, Tom checked his Deringers, one in each vest pocket. They were Colt No. 2 'New Deringers,' single-shot, .41 caliber. Tom had a satisfied feeling that he would be back together that very day with the woman he loved and adored.

Lizzie Wyllie lay dozing, alone in the room, early Monday afternoon. A noise at the door woke her. A man and woman with pleasant voices laughed and called out "Western Union Express!" It took Lizzie a minute or two to rise and falter toward the door, and by then the couple were gone. She saw a small envelope on the floor, the kind telegrams came in. She picked it up and went to the light at the window to open it.

My God, she thought, *finally something from Kate and John!*

When she read the note, she dropped her hands in bitter disappointment at the irony. She was past tears. All this for nothing! She could have stayed in Michigan and had an abortion instead of all this posing and lying and dirtiness, just to wind up half-dead and miserable, with nothing to show for it. What drove it home was that she recognized the handwriting—it wasn't John's. It was Kate Morgan's, who was being dishonest as always. Why was she writing for John? Had John left town already to go back to his wife? Was anyone really even coming for her tonight? Should she try to leave now, rather than wait for the noose to tighten—or was Kate really going to come with John to get her? Or maybe Kate was sending John, and then bugging out on both of them to leave them in the lurch. Lizzie's thinking wasn't clear enough to make heads or tails of her dilemma.

All she had now was a final, depressed resolve. She had made a botch of her life, and was destroying the poor thing growing inside of her. She determined she was going to kill herself, the baby, and the man who had betrayed her. And Kate Morgan, if possible. It wasn't revenge—it was justice. It was preventing these depraved people from hurting anyone else. The great irony was that, had she kept the baby, the child would have been the one person who would be with her always. The world had taken the first one from her, and now she was again betrayed. To do what she had decided yesterday, on the beach with Frank, she would make one final trip across the Bay into San Diego. She dropped Kate's note into the fire, where it folded up like an autumn leaf, blackening as if in proof of Kate's evil, and consumed in a brightening of the yellow-orange flame. With its rising smoke fled the last ounce of trust Lizzie had in Kate, and the last shred of love she felt for John. She loved her mother and sister too much to return to them in this ruined state. They would be better off without her.

In the early afternoon, Lizzie set out on her journey. She was so sick she could hardly walk. For the first time, she went by the front desk without asking for the imaginary doctor and his imaginary wife—Kate and John, who had never come for her, and the devil might care if they ever did.

The light was gray and dismal outside, as a weak Lizzie walked slowly to the street and waited for a trolley. The conductor had to help her on board. The steam-powered trolley rolled slowly through a darkening Coronado. Storm clouds were rolling in. The air was disturbed, and horses acted skittish. Dogs and cats slunk for cover.

It was a rough crossing on the great steel boat that carried people and horse carriages. The water was choppy. It was windy and chilly, and people were bundled up. Lizzie shivered in her shawl.

As the boat rocked with an ominous threat of violence to come, she saw a huge black wall of storm clouds approaching from the southwest.

On the San Diego side, a man helped Lizzie up onto the dock. She paid a man with a carriage to take her up D Street. She half drowsed as the horse's hooves steadily clip-clopped on the concrete pavement littered with horse manure. He let her off on Fifth Street. She knew exactly what she wanted to do here.

Tom Morgan took only about twenty minutes to reach the inexpensive hotel where Wyatt Earp had told him Kate and her companion were staying. He walked calmly into the lobby and spoke to an elderly concierge who looked up, over half-rim glasses, from the newspaper he was reading. "Good day, Sir. Need a room before it rains?"

No thanks," Tom said carefully. "I'm looking for some friends of mine, whom I would like to invite to dinner. She's a dark-haired, strong looking woman with a pleasant face and striking eyes. He's a handsome man with a mustache, about so high—?" Tom raised his hand to his shoulder.

The concierge nodded. "Sounds like Mr. and Mrs. Lomax. The Lomaxes." He turned and looked at the key board. "Doug and Claire Lomax, in Room 15 upstairs. Would you like me to show you up there?"

"No, thanks, no need to trouble yourself."

"On the second floor then," said the concierge, pointing to a wooden staircase wending out of sight from the carpeted and ornately furnished, rather cluttered little lobby.

"Thank you very kindly," Tom said. He debated—should he wait in the shadows? Afraid to miss her and lose her again, he bounded up the stairs, ready for anything. His guns were ready. He feared no man. Walking down the narrow, carpeted hallway, he came to the reddish, shellacked door of Room 15. He put his ear to the door and listened for a minute or two. He wondered if they were in. He didn't hear Kate's voice, nor a man's. Then he heard a faint clinking sound, like glass on glass. A smell of beer and cigar smoke wafted through the key hole. That did it. Tom knocked.

"Yeah?" said a man's voice.

"Mr. Lomax? I have a message for you."

"Gimme a second."

Tom heard a crashing, stumbling sound. Feet shuffled on a linoleum floor. A chain lock rattled, and the door opened a few inches. An unshaven man in his 30s stared out with bloodshot eyes. "Yeah?"

"I have some money for you, Mr. Lomax."

"Hold it a moment." The chain rattled as he released it, and he opened the door. "You from Western Union?"

"Something like that." Tom stepped inside. "Where's Kate?"

"What?"

Tom had sized him up—a tough guy, but a city type, without a farm boy's brawn and sinew. Tom shoved him lightly away from the door, and slipped the door shut behind him. "If you have a gun," Tom said, "don't pull it out. I've got two guns, and I'll plug you before you can roll those drunken eyes twice in your skull. Where is she?"

"Who?"

Tom slapped him across the face, and the man fell down against the bed in the middle of the room. "I'm not going to ask you twice." He pulled out one of his Deringers. "If you lie to me, or lead me on, I'll put lead in your skull. Do you understand me, fool?"

The man staggered to a table covered with beer bottles and slumped in the chair. This man wasn't going to fight anyone. He mumbled something slurry in a disgruntled, fuzzy voice.

Tom held the Deringer and lifted the man erect by his soiled shirt back with his free hand. "One more time, before I throw you out the window. Where is Kate, my wife?"

John Longfield held up his hands defensively. He slurred: "Meeting 'm in back Hotel del Coronado after midnight."

"Who is them?'

"Claire and Lizzie. Kate, I mean, and Lizzie."

"This must be another of Kate's schemes. Who's she blackmailing now?"

"Spreckels."

"The rich guy? She's lost her mind for sure." Tom saw he must save Kate from herself. "Are you sure about this? What is your name?"

"John Longfield. Doug Lomax, husband of Claire Lomax. You?"

"Tom Morgan, her real husband. I've come to get her back. When is she coming back to this room?" He released his grip on the man's shirt, and John Longfield slumped with lolling head.

"Isn't," Longfield slurred. Gesturing drunkenly, he pulled his watch from his pocket and showed it to Tom. "Midnight, hotel."

The thought of this drunk's hands on Kate nearly made Tom shoot him, but Tom thought of the concierge and the mess that would cause. Prudently, he pocketed his Deringer. "You got any whiskey?"

Longfield pointed to a dark area under the bed. Tom reached underneath and pulled out a bottle of Red Canary. "That's good stuff. Let's split a glass before I go."

"Delighted," John said, lolling around.

Tom poured himself a glass and pushed the bottle across. "Help yourself."

Longfield grabbed the bottle and upended it in a generous swig.

"That's right," Tom said. He rose and pushed his untouched glass to Longfield. "You should have a few more."

Tom let himself out of the room. His last view of Longfield was as the man poured himself another shot, and almost missed the glass. He wouldn't be going anywhere with Kate tonight. As far as Tom was concerned, he hoped Longfield would drink himself into a coma this evening so he wouldn't warn Kate.

Tom went down the stairs, thanked the concierge, and left the building. He knew where the ferry landing was. He would head there later this evening. First, he must go to his hotel room, have a bit to eat, rest a little, and then pack his belongings.

After giving the note to the young couple who would deliver it to Lizzie, Kate walked back toward Date Street. Her path took her by the railroad station, and there she saw two men who looked like detectives looking at a police sketch—of Lizzie. The town was swarming with people paid to secretly protect John Spreckels, and he could easily pay an army if need be. Instead of numbers, he had brains on his side, the best in the business. Time to get out of town, and not a moment too soon.

When Kate arrived at the hotel room, John Longfield lay on the bed, passed out. The table was covered with empty beer bottles and an upended whiskey bottle. Looked like he'd tied one on. One side of his face had a welt on it, and his eye socket was turning purple.

She shook him. "John! John! Wake up. We've got to get out of town."

"Tom Morgan," John said in a slurry voice with his head hanging to one side and his cheeks rubbery. His eyes fluttered.

"Oh my God," Kate said. "Was Tom here? Did he hit you?"

John couldn't raise his head, but he brought up one hand, the fingers in the shape of a gun. "Had Deringer."

"That's Tom," she said. "Did you tell him anything?"

"Told him midnight at the Del."

"How could you?"

"Had Deringer." John lifted the two fingers again, face down on the table. She started to protest, but he raised himself up and said more lucidly: "I was afraid he was going to stay here waiting for you, so I told him that to get him out of here."

"You should have said we were meeting her in New York in Times Square," Kate yelled, throwing her purse at the wall. She stormed down the hall to the bathroom so she wouldn't do something to him. She made up her mind that she was going to lose John Longfield at the first opportunity. But she still needed him for the moment. And she was pretty soft on him.

When she returned to the room, he lay sprawled and snoring on the bed. She gently put a coverlet over him. He had never raised a hand to her, not even while plastered, and she like that about him.

Kate agitatedly walked up and down the room. What to do now? It would be too risky to try and reach the Hotel del Coronado before Tom did. She was frightened enough of him to not want to go in the first place, knowing he was there. With any luck, Tom would be stuck on the island all night. Ferry service ended in the early evening, and she hoped it would shut down a little earlier in anticipation of the storm. He would go there, look for Kate, and not find her. He might see Lizzie outside but would not recognize her. She thought: *Maybe I can escape from Tom if I go to Canada*.

Lottie A. Bernard entered Chick's Gun Shop on Fifth Street in San Diego, and walked stiffly to the counter. Several onlookers watched, and they would testify. Mrs. Bernard spoke with Chick in a conversation that lasted a few minutes. Chick handed her an unloaded gun. She held it, gave it back, and asked if it would be hard to use. Chick showed her how to point it, and how to pull the trigger. With the cylinder empty, he aimed at the floor and pulled the trigger for her several times. She nodded and pushed a handful of dollar bills across the counter.

At her request, Chick loaded five rounds into the cylinder, and put the gun into a shoe box. She had purchased a rather ungainly weapon, a cheap throw-away with rust on it, known as an American Bulldog. That wasn't a brand name, but a type. It was a cheap knock-off of the British Bulldog, the much-imitated civilian version of the British Army's Webley service revolver. The usual Bulldog was a .32 caliber with a six shot cylinder, but this .45 version had an usual five-round cylinder because the rounds were longer than the gun's design called for. It made for a deceptively large looking cannon of a gun. Chick wrapped the box in brown gift paper and tied it with sturdy string. He slid it across the counter to her with words of thanks. She picked up her package from the counter, and hobbled out the door.

A bystander commented to Chick: "That woman is going to hurt herself with that thing."

Chick shrugged. A sale was a sale. What she did was no business of his.

Waiting for John to sober up, Kate walked through the Stingaree on a mission—to learn how much the Pinkertons actually knew about her, if anything. She walked through the red light district, retracing her steps of a few days ago when she'd trailed the Bowler Pinkerton agent. Her mind raced with plans and counter-plans. She walked obliviously through the bedlam of drunks, gamblers, prostitutes, Chinese laundrymen and tong assassins, delivery boys on bicycles, gunslingers, Mexican cowboys in sombreros toting steel, madams leering from open windows, and all the rest of the colorful Stingaree. It was getting cold and drizzly. She pulled her shawl tightly around her shoulders, with her arms wrapped protectively around herself under that, as if to protect and isolate herself from the mayhem all around. Not that it would help if a bottle or knife happened to come flying her way. She kept her hat low over her forehead as she passed through that same alley again. She stood across from the Pinkerton building, a two-story Spanish-Mexican mission-style building with a flat roof and yellowish stucco surfaces. As Kate stood watching the building, she saw a slow but constant stream of people come and go. It was a hive of activity, and Kate understood why. She could be sure that almost none of the people coming and going had any real grasp of the case they were part of. Spreckels'

people would use extreme discretion. The left hand would not know what the right was doing.

A woman agent disguised in maid's dress was just coming out in the company of a Pinkerton agent who shifted his walking stick from one hand to the other as he pulled out his watch fob, and as he looked at the time, Kate saw a Pinkerton badge by the watch, confirming they were agents. Kate stepped into a general store nearby, found a section with uniforms, and emerged not long after wearing a starchy little white domestic's cap on her head. She had worn such things often enough. With feigned surety and casualness, she crossed the street and entered the Pinkerton building.

Kate walked along a smoky corridor where she heard people's voices in conversation and typewriters clattering. She ducked into someone's empty office, picked up a box of papers, and made herself look as if she were on official business as she walked through the building. She looked around and then ascended a winding stairway at the end of a corridor. Emerging on the second floor, she walked calmly but purposefully as if she belonged there. A man nodded to her, and she nodded back with an efficient little smile she hoped was agent-like.

Kate saw a door marked *Supervisor*, which was partly open. On the wall just outside this door was a cork board with papers tacked to it. Some were Wanted posters, others telegrams or notes. She heard men talking inside the room. "Hotel del Coronado," she heard, and other snatches of conversation wafted out: "money" and "girl" and "Room 302." She heard enough to know they were working her case in that very room. Standing at the cork board, as if doing some legitimate task, Kate spied a blackboard in a wooden frame inside the room. It was on wheels, and on it was chalked writing—telling her this was the planning and staging room for the Spreckels case. She'd found the Lottie A. Bernard headquarters.

Two men in heated conversation came out, one of them smoking a cigar. Kate reached up to the cork bulletin board and rattled one of the papers as if on business. The two men, who looked like high officials, walked past her with furrowed brows and preoccupied looks, and continued their conversation as they strode away. "Another day or two, that's all we need," one said to the other.

Kate thought: *You are so right about that!* She looked left and right. A young female with rolls of paper under her arms passed but didn't pay attention to the domestic standing by the cork board. Kate ducked into the office and pushed the door shut.

Seeing a large black steel safe, she noticed its door was not quite locked. In their haste and argument, the two Pinkertons had left it ajar. She pulled the heavy door open, glanced at the piled papers, and saw the money. She quickly scooped what looked like a thousand dollars in tens and twenties into her pockets. Her heart beat fast and hard now that she had a payoff.

She rifled through papers piled on a desk and a table. She saw diagrams of the Hotel Del, with Lizzie's room circled. She saw surveillance sketches of Lizzie...*Too much!* They had pictures of Lizzie talking with some shoeless man on the beach. Lizzie being ferried around town, smiling, by a boy in a carriage. Lizzie having tea and a bun in the hotel restaurant.

Kate blanched at seeing a sketch of herself, talking with Wyatt Earp outside the Yuma Building. She closed her eyes and shuddered deeply. She fingered the locket at her neck. The noose was already tightening. And there was a copy of Tom Morgan's photo from the telegraph office. They had photographs and sketches, of other people she didn't recognize, so they had not quite put the case together yet. The detective she'd overheard estimated they were two days from solving their case. *I'll be out of town by then*, Kate thought, *vanished without a trace, like a ghost*.

She heard voices drawing near, so she ducked behind the door with her heart pounding and the arteries in her neck drumming into her throbbing ears. What if they were to walk in now and catch her here? It would all be over—she'd get decades in prison, or worse. She stiffened and prepared for the worst. But the voices passed outside and receded down the corridor. She released a huge lungful of pent air. Slowly, her heart and ears and neck stopped feeling constricted, and the pounding died away.

In this silence, standing at the heart of the Pinkerton case, she pulled the blackboard closer. She piled all their papers up high on a table and on chairs. Nearby stood an ashtray, beside a humidor and smoking supplies, including matches. Kate lit a large, pungent cigar, got it going nicely, and buried it in the papers. The crisp smell of burning paper told her the fire was pulling nicely.

She opened a supply cabinet and saw a bottle of rubber cement. That would be nicely and highly flammable. She opened it and set it right near the papers. Smoky flames were just starting to lightly rise as she slipped outside. She locked the door from outside and threw the key into a dark corner as she sauntered to the stairs.

As she headed down the stairs, she pulled on the little red lever of an electrically operated fire alarm system. Bells began ringing all over the building. People looked puzzled as they stepped out of offices and stood around looking at each other.

The weight of the money felt good in her pockets. It took Kate about two minutes to step out the front door and start across the street, which was shrouded in fast-moving waves of drizzle and fog. As she stepped onto the opposite curb, she heard shouts and yells on the second floor. The fire would not hurt or kill anyone, but would incinerate the Pinkertons' evidence in an accident apparently caused by a careless smoker.

It mattered little in several ways as time marched on. The Pinkertons would orchestrate a cover-up designed to protect John Spreckels from any hint of scandal. The Hawai'ian monarchy would be overthrown by U.S. and European corporate opportunists just six weeks later, led by Pineapple King Sanford Dole. The redoubtable Claus Spreckels would lose his sugar cane plantations and all interest in the Hawai'ian state as a government hostile to him took over, under U.S. management and protected by the U.S. Marines. Claus would move his operations to the region around Monterey, California, where a town named Spreckels would grow up, and a new era in his sugar empire would dawn—fueled by sugar beets instead of cane. People like Spreckels always landed on their feet.

Kate returned to the hotel room to find John Longfield sitting on the bed, holding his head. He had made some coffee, and the room was filled with its good aroma. "If you pull another stunt like that, I'm throwing you out," she told him.

"I'm sorry." He held his head and winced. "Never again."

"That's what they all say. Here, I brought us something to eat." She had picked up a light dinner of sandwiches in wax paper bags in a restaurant along the way. "We're pulling out, John. The Pinkertons are on our heels, and my husband is in town looking for me."

"And Lizzie?"

"I don't know. I've set them back a bit, but we don't have a minute to lose. We have to try to get Lizzie out tomorrow. Tom will go to the hotel and not recognize her and he won't see me. He may come back here looking for me..." She stopped and calculated. "Yes, he'll know during the middle of the night that I won't be there. He'll be in a rage because he'll figure I tricked him. He won't recognize Lizzie, so they'll pass each other in the night. Tom will take the first ferry back in the morning. The peninsular road will probably be flooded. I don't think he'll be able to rent a horse from anyone to ride the twenty miles or whatever it is along the beach. He'll come straight here, but we'll be gone, and I'll leave a false forwarding address. We've still got to get my trunk out of Los Angeles."

"And Lizzie's trunks are here in town. I have the baggage claim checks."

"Don't you dare go anywhere near that depot right now. We have to wait for it all to cool off. And besides, her trunks are high and dry there for the time being. Where would we put them?"

John nibbled at his sandwich and sipped coffee, slurping and blinking. "When do we leave here?"

"In the morning. We'll wait, out of sight. When we see him get off the ferry and head for our hotel, we'll get on board when it's safe. We'll cross over to Coronado, get Lizzie, and take the beach train back into town the long way. Or maybe I'll hire a carriage to take us north to Del Mar to catch the train, avoiding San Diego altogether." She sighed deeply. "I'm tired. Let's get a good night's sleep, and be well rested in the morning. Promise me, John, please, that you'll behave yourself from here on."

"I'm sorry. I will be good, I swear it."

"Yeah, like you swore to spend May's money on Lizzie's abortion, and a thousand other things. You are enough to drive a woman crazy." She rubbed her hand in his hair. "But you are far more loveable than Tom."

Tom checked out of the Hotel Brewster and walked, with his bag in hand, down to the ferry dock. He just caught the last ferry across. It was a gray and blustery crossing as darkness fell early. Drizzle and fog moved this way and that in a growing, knife-like wind. Icy, gritty gusts slashed left and right in unpredictable turns. Tom huddled, thinking, on a bench in the large common hall on the top deck. He planned to rent a horse and buggy tomorrow morning, once he had Kate with him, and ride with her to the train station. There was little for him to do in San Diego. He'd talk her into moving to Chicago or someplace with excitement and action. This was no place for her either—just a quiet backwater except for that teeming red light district that belonged in a city ten times the size of San Diego. Whatever this crazy scheme of hers, she might come away with a nice sum of money. He couldn't wait to have her in bed with him. The ferry churned and rocked on the foamy Bay waters as the lights of Coronado drew near.

A monstrous storm cloud like a black wall, an animal with claws, at least a mile high and hundreds of miles wide, rolled toward landfall in Southern California as night fell. Lizzie had her purse, and the gun in it, as she stood with other guests on a balcony to see the storm approach. It seemed a fitting end to a stormy saga and a depressing tragedy. Harry West spoke with her briefly before he went home—he asked about her, and warned her that nobody really knew how this new hotel would endure such a terrible storm. Windows on the sea side were being boarded up, and guests were being moved to the street side just in case. With myriad little lanterns and many windows, the great white building with its brick-red turrets looked like a newly launched ship about to test itself in one of the century's worst storms.

Scared but intrigued hotel guests huddled together on balconies for a view, as if at a racing event. Dressed in warm coats and hats, they sipped hot drinks and looked toward the monster bearing down on them. Then, as night fell, people went off to eat. They were bored with waiting. The barometric pressure dropped, and Lizzie's head felt light. She took the last of her laudanum, welcoming its herbal bite and then the numbness. There was no way back; no way forward. Her guts felt as if they were on fire.

The balconies were empty, as the wind began to howl. Shotguns of sleet and hail slammed against the windows and their wooden coverings on the sea side. The storm grew ever more furious. From time to time, one heard the pop of a window here or there, sucked out and burst by low pressure, or gripped by the cooling and contraction of the building. Dropping glass tinkled along the hotel's outside walls and rattled on concrete walks. Even as the shards fell, they were spun and twirled by the lashing rain.

Lizzie kept her shawl around her shoulders as she wandered around the common areas of the great hotel. She went to her room to doze for a few hours. Not long before midnight, she rose and dressed. She wore her sealskin jacket and the shawl over that. What a shame that she had never gotten any of her nice clothes out of the trunks. No matter now.

A shadowy female shape, hunched in pain, she walked slowly down the deserted hallways. The hotel was sparsely populated because of its remoteness and the economic disaster that had devastated San Diego since 1889. She walked down to the first floor and saw that its carpeted emptiness was silent as in a church by night. She continued down the stairs, into the corridors under the ground, and up a flight of stairs to the rear of the hotel. The storm raged outside. Wind howled like an army at war, complete with the artillery flashes of lightning and the boom of thunder. She came to the open door and tried peering outside. She doubted if John cared enough about her to come in this mess to get her. After all, Kate had to fake notes from him to Lizzie. She felt the sting of cold, and the biting pangs in her belly, and thought it was the fetus clawing at her in pain and protest. What fear she felt relented to angry resignation. She didn't cry—she was past all that. She was drained of emotion, and scarce on reason. She had her glasses in her purse, but didn't bother wearing them. If he were looking for her, let him find her, instead of always the other way around. She was done with that.

Hearing sweet, strong chimes—as the metal works and steel hammers of a clock rang quarter to midnight, in that little ditty of Big Ben notes—Tom Morgan rose from the deep, comfortable arm chair in which he had been sitting for some time. It was located in the guts of the Hotel del Coronado, in an area near the main lobby from where he could watch people coming and going. He had dozed a little when the hallway fell silent and nobody came along. Now he was awake. The new-fangled electric lights burned soft and steady as you pleased, and made for an oddly comforting, safe feeling. Not that Tom wanted to feel comfortable or safe. He wanted Kate, and she had not appeared. He was beginning to get angry. Was she pulling a terrible trick on him? Was she getting back at him somehow? In the silence, his mind began to launch conspiracies, one after the other. No, she wouldn't be that cruel. Then again, Kate had a streak, maybe cruel, certainly unfeeling. She could walk over corpses without blinking, as the Germans around Hamburg, Iowa would say in their accents. What about this damned guy she was with? That drunken slob did look like a city con man. Maybe the plan was to have him come instead and shoot Tom in the back. He felt his vest pockets and made sure his Deringers were ready and loaded. In that rain outside, he must keep his pistols dry.

Tom Morgan walked cautiously and quietly through the subterranean corridors of the hotel. There! A woman's ghostly figure walked through the bowels of the hotel. It could only be Kate!

She disappeared around a bend in the underground passage, where store windows gleamed dully in the night. He came to a small flight of steps leading upward to an open door. No sight of her. Was she leading him on? Did she have that drunkard lying in wait to kill him? His paranoia fueled rage as he knotted his fist around a Deringer.

Wind and rain blew in relentlessly. The gale outside howled. He walked up the stairs and out to the edge of the rain. He felt betrayed, sent here on a fool's errand. Kate had seen his photographs, and decided to send him in one direction while she and her worthless lover-boy vanished in the opposite direction. She'd be halfway to Los

Angeles by now. He almost cried with the terrible, overpowering rage that gripped him.

Standing in the open French doors, he saw the woman again.

Kate! So was it a trick, or wasn't it?

She stood outside, at the bottom of the steps below leading down to the beach sand. She was looking out toward the black, roiling sea. White crests by the hundred ran like wild horses panicked by constant lightning. Low pressure lifted the sea in a monstrous curve like a pregnant woman's belly. Unthinkable powers raged and thundered, moving boulders under the water as if they were pebbles, rattling like gravel. The world was coming apart. The hotel would surely be torn apart any moment now like paper in mad hands.

Tom stared at the woman. From behind, sopping in the rain, she looked just like Kate. It must be her. Maybe the head, the height, the hair were a little different—or she looked different because he had not seen her in years, or he didn't remember her as she was, but he was overcome by a mix of overwhelming emotions as he started to open her mouth to call her name. "Kate!"

Somewhere behind Lizzie, inside the hotel, one of the clocks struck twelve times. The long, slow tolling of hammer on gong, heavy steel on heavy steel, sounded like a summons to a funeral—her own. It was midnight—the time Kate had said to meet her and John behind the hotel. Lizzie stood trembling on the steps outside, holding her purse in both hands. In the purse was the heavy gun. Wind whipped her this way and that. Her hair was plastered wetly around her skull. The wind seemed to want to tear off what little clothing she had. It moved her around in little steps. Her clothing was soaked, and she trembled with a chill. She felt utterly drained of any hope, any emotion, even of thought. She rode a nightmare of pure instinct.

Long seething white breakers came thundering up the shore like express trains, crashing against boulders. The ground shook under her feet.

Lightning flashed as the storm grew ever more powerful. Maenads howled in the night, and lightning gave sickly flashes that were followed by growls of thunder. The storm grew ever more terrifying on her numbed senses and chilled body. This must be the doorway to Hell.

She dropped her purse as she held the gun in both trembling hands. Her hair blew back and forth across her face, and buckets of rain slammed against her from all sides. The rain seemed sinuous and alive as it wrapped itself around her in violent seduction.

Lightning made claw marks in the sky and tortured her figure with cold light. Standing on a small flight of concrete steps near the beach sand, with the sea just a few yards away, she raised the gun in both hands. She had figured out that she would put the gun high up in the roof in back of her mouth and aim at the center of her brain. That was the surest and quickest way to end everything for herself and the child. Already she could taste metal, like blood, and smell machine oil. Her hands trembled as she tried to tighten her grip and position her finger on the trigger.

Lightning and thunder crescendoed.

She heard a man's voice. John! So he'd come after all. What was he shouting? She lowered the gun and turned.

Yelling "Kate! Oh my God! My darling Kate!" Tom bounded across the walkway toward a spooky, sopping figure with rain-flat hair who stood looking toward the sea. "Kate!" As he reached the top of the steps, she turned.

The face looking up at him was pale as a fish's belly, with the same sickly, slimy gray color. Her cheeks might be covered in fine scales, for all he knew, or were those droplets of water? Her eye sockets were bony, her eyes and mouth nocturnal holes. Her mouth hung open and her features rippled with exaggerated emotions. This was a monster in a nightmare. Was she a thing that had come out of the sea? He stood frozen with fear and wonder. No, it was Kate for sure.

She raised a gun at him with both hands, and the muzzle flashed. He heard the pop and felt something whiz by his head. She wanted to kill him. Why, Kate? He couldn't be sure—the face looked distorted and grotesque with emotions in a lightning flash. Her gaze was large and luminous, almost supernatural. Her eyes were so wide he saw white all around the pupils. Thunder growled warnings and threats.

She'd lured him here to kill him.

That did it. Tom felt slammed by adrenalin, and cross-current emotions as if he were drunk. He reached into his vest pocket in one sweeping motion, took out a Deringer, and went down the steps in a second, maybe two. She fired again, but her gun was a piece of junk that fizzled and failed to shoot properly. He put the muzzle of his Deringer to her right temple and squeezed the trigger. In the muzzle flash, muffled by rain and wind, he saw that it was not Kate at all, but some crazed dark-haired girl who looked a bit like her. Tom pocketed his gun and ran. He had not meant to kill the girl, but she had tried to shoot him—why? He would never understand.

Thus, Tom Morgan disappeared into the night and into history.

He left behind him Lizzie Wyllie, now dead, the supposed Lottie Bernard. Rain and wind whipped her lifeless figure as she lay face up. Her face looked indistinct—veiled in shadow, one side blackened with powder residue, the other pale as a porcelain angel's, enigmatic but peaceful. The gun lay on the step under a blackened, dangling hand that would never grasp again. The storm buffeted her body with passionate lust. Gradually, the residue washed away, leaving a pale, sleeping angel.

The storm abated before dawn. Only a mute fog remained, penetrating everywhere. Electric lights glowed like luminous cotton balls, and the eaves dripped noisily all around. Here and there lay broken glass, but the great resort hotel had survived its first typhoon.

The body lay as she had fallen during the night. An electrician named Cone moved wraithlike through the fog on his morning rounds to trim the lights. He stopped and at first thought she was a mannequin lying on her back on the steps. Then he saw the gun by her right hand, the empty gaze, the gory hole in her right temple. He bent down with horror written on his face, and lightly slapped her cheek. "Ma'am! Lady! You have to wake up. Please wake up. Oh my God, you're not sleeping. You're—oh my God, oh my God..."

Cone ran to fetch help, and a saga was launched that would take the nation by storm, and be remembered for generations.

11. Conspiracy's End—Legend's Start

Kate and John heard the near-hysterical rumors and gossip about the beautiful woman found dead across the bay, and knew it was Lizzie. They need not bother crossing. Poor Lizzie would now tell no tales, and Kate was eager to get far away from Tom. John grew misty-eyed, but Kate comforted him: "She's an angel in heaven now, Johnny."

Days later, Kate and John sat together in Third Class as a train clattered eastward. She had plenty of money from the Pinkerton safe, but would not tell him about it. She always bought him cigars and a little beer at train stops, and he seemed contented. They enjoyed a mild midmorning sunshine under blue skies in the California desert. The black locomotive lustily pulled dozens of passenger and cargo cars while emitting a long plume of dark gray smoke.

John, dressed in his dark suit and slouch hat, sat dozing against Kate. She wore a wide-brimmed straw hat and a tan outfit with black trim and buttons. Feeling his strong body against her, she did some careful calculations. She thought ahead, planning to lose him, but for a while she would continue enjoying him. She'd keep him under her thumb, feeding him sex candy, until she was safely far away from Southern California. Her main concern now was that her trunk was still at the Grants' house in Los Angeles. Actually, she reflected, her main concern was that she'd been so close to Tom. More than anything, she needed to put distance between herself and Tom, the more the better, so she could stop looking over her shoulder so much. Maybe she would disappear into Canada.

Kate read the newspapers and was able to follow the story in San Diego minutely, as it was telegraphed in breathless relays to all parts of the United States. The main source of information were the Spreckels-owned and controlled newspapers in San Diego, and Kate knew they were doctoring information to protect the owner of the Hotel del Coronado.

When the body was found by an electrician, the coroner's people came across within two hours to collect it. She was still thought to be Mrs. Lottie A. Bernard. Her stay had been a mysterious one, with many questions being asked, but it took a week or two to realize Lottie A. Bernard was a fiction. Then, for a period of some days, there was absolute certainty she had been a gorgeous and stylish runaway from Detroit named Lizzie Wyllie, whose grieving mother and sister identified her for certain from a coroner's description and a police sketch circulating throughout the country. Kate only barely recognized her—the beautiful hair had been cropped after death, and the corpse had been embalmed after some amount of deterioration. To Kate's relief, the identity kept changing as new leads poured in. For a time, police thought she was a Katie Logan who had worked for the Grants in Los Angeles. Alas, that meant never being able to get her trunk out. But the next bit of news made up for all of that.

Finally, someone notified San Diego police it might have been Kate Morgan. As Kate read this, in a train station near Omaha, she glowed with joy. Here was her opportunity to escape responsibility for the botched blackmail attempt. On the one hand, the national media made a circus of her name, which she could never use again. On the other hand, as it now seemed she was officially dead, she could reincarnate herself in any of her many aliases, and live a new life free as a bird. The Spreckels Machine were only too glad to spread dark rumors to tarnish Kate and Tom Morgan in a cover-up. If someone had a brain, Kate thought, they could put the clues together. Mrs. Wyllie swore it was her daughter, dead and lost to her. The press reported that Katie Logan had babbled to someone that her real name was Lizzie. The hankies in her room said *Lizzie Anderson*, but the coroner misread it as *Little Anderson*. The hankies in Kate's trunk in Los Angeles were embroidered *Louisa Anderson*, but it appeared the fools in charge of the world were so busy creating elusive fantasies that nobody thought the case through. Gradually, Kate began breathing easier. In a way, it was like threatening the Toad she'd rat on him, and getting paid off, as with all the other stupid men she'd blackmailed. She was going to get away with this, and she'd learned some valuable lessons. She'd never work with others again, nor use any name more than once.

Poor Lizzie lay in state like a dead princess at Johnson & Company Mortuary in San Diego, while breathless rumors and stories about her swirled across the nation. No doubt fueled by Pinkerton's and

Spreckels' sources, the rumors told of her shady dealings, her hushed sex scandals involving the high and mighty, her husband's disgraceful cardsharping, and so on. Even as Lizzie became ever more disgraced as a Ruined Woman, a perverse romantic sense raised her to the saintly status of Fallen Angel. A Ruined Woman could be a whore or an adulteress, and fie on her—but, in the romantic version, she could be an innocent angel brought low by the evils of men and the world. Apparently, as Kate saw in the newspaper accounts, the women of San Diego, and of the nation, felt the latter was the case. San Diego's women, dressed in their finest, thronged by the thousands to visit their Fallen Angel every day and converse endlessly as if visiting with relatives. In the end, after a solemn high church funeral, she was sent off on a donkey cart, in a plain wooden box, driven by some old man who'd been given a coin to get drunk on later. She was dropped in a hole at Mount Hope Cemetery, without a marker, and forgotten as quickly as the dirt started hitting her coffin.

K ate mulled her options as they rode east toward Cleveland. As she remarked to John, "If Kate Morgan lies dead in San Diego, and if I never use my name again, I can put this whole thing behind me."

"What name would you use?" John asked innocently, smoking a cigarette, legs crossed, just making conversation.

She looked at him and realized she would never tell him. She had not even made up a new name, but she would never again make the mistake of sharing it with an accomplice. "Maybe I'll go by Lizzie Wyllie for a while." He looked startled, she grinned as if it were just a joke, and he shrugged carelessly and looked out the window while enjoying his smoke.

John and Kate changed trains regularly over several days. At one point, John said: "Poor Lizzie. What will I tell her mother? Her sister?"

She said: "We'll be in Cleveland soon. You'll mail your wife that you are still looking for work, as you did before we left for California with Lizzie. Make sure nobody can find your address in Cleveland. We'll stay there together for a little while, and you can have me all to yourself. Tell her you think you'll have work soon, and, oh by the way, you heard about Lizzie—the rumors are all false. There is nothing to it. She...has...let's see...she has run away. She is living happily in Toronto and never plans to visit Detroit again, nor does she ever want to see her family again."

"Nobody'll believe it. Everyone knows she loved her mother and sister, and they loved her."

"Lizzie will never return to them, so it doesn't matter. It's nice to think that Lizzie still lives, in her fashion—in some ghostly way, in her mother's and sister's faith and hopes. It will give them hope, even if it's a cruel hope that ends in disappointment." Kate grinned. " I died on the beach that night in the great storm—and am a ghost now, a ghost of me, but people will say I am the ghost of the Hotel del Coronado, when it's really Lizzie."

"That's pretty rich." John put his arm around her. *Poor Lizzie*, he thought. *Nice Kate.*

She told John: "Soon, you'll go back to your wife and kids. You'll put all this behind you. You'll tell them Lizzie went her way, and lives in Toronto, and you will go back to your life and be happy."

John laid a furtive hand on her thigh. "I can't get enough of you."

She patted his hand. "It'll wear off. Love and sex always do." She nuzzled a kiss behind his ear. "You flatter me though. I'll stay with you in Cleveland for a bit. We'll have fun together. You won't get lonely or bored, and I'll keep you out of trouble. When the dust has settled, you'll go back to Detroit, and I will get on a train and vanish."

John said: "Like a ghost."

 END

Author's Notes

I have published a nonfictional, scholarly analysis of the so-called Kate Morgan story, titled <u>Dead Move: Kate Morgan and the Haunting Mystery of Coronado</u>—that is the first of two books in this volume.

The second book in this volume is a novel—<u>Lethal Journey</u>, an 1892 noir period piece. Lethal Journey is a gaslight mystery, closely based on <u>Dead Move</u> in almost every regard except one.

In <u>Dead Move</u>, I lay out my theory about what really happened. It is very close to the gripping drama in this book in most points, but not all. One major difference is that, while Tom Morgan as a character has no importance in my nonfiction analysis, legend has made of him the larger than life villain you find in this novel. Legend has it that Kate Morgan died at the hotel, not Lizzie. As you can see in this book and in my other book, I believe it was Lizzie Wyllie who died at the Hotel del Coronado on that fateful night in November 1892. I have thoroughly documented and detailed my theory in <u>Dead Move</u>.

That title, by the way, came to me courtesy a friend of mine, who was a manager at the hotel. I worked at the hotel as a part-time shuttle driver for several years, and one day in 2006 I asked him, jokingly, if he'd experienced any ghostly activities lately. He said a lady had only a few days earlier checked in, and light-heartedly asked to be put in Room 3327. People often do this, to challenge the ghost legend. That was once Room 302, in which Lottie A. Bernard was staying at the time of her death.

The hotel's policy, in modern times, has been to only rent that room out if it is the last room available, or if a guest specifically asks for it. In either case, the desk clerks are to tell the guest that the room is said to be haunted, and to proceed with that caution in mind. The lady called the front desk after midnight, as many people before her have, and demanded to immediately be moved to another room as far from there as possible. As my friend explained to me, moving guests and their luggage to another room, without re-registering them, is called a 'dead move' in hotel parlance. I thought it was a fitting element for a gripping title. The most famous dead move occurred in 1983, in connection with another haunted room (3519) that is sometimes connected with the Kate Morgan (or Lizzie Wyllie) ghost story. Vice President George H. W. Bush was staying at the hotel, and one of his Secret Service officers was housed in Room 3519. The agent called the front desk in the middle of the night, asking them to tell the people above him to stop loudly talking and walking around. They informed him he was directly under the roof, and only pigeons could be walking around. This strong and fearless public servant demanded an immediate dead move. I imagine he was already outside the room with his gun and luggage as the bellhops came running.

The terrible storm, which so dramatically underscores the ending, really happened—exactly as described. People called it the storm of the century. On that terrible night, the drama of Lottie A. Bernard did really reach its dark finale with the sound of gunfire. There are some major differences, however, between this novel and my nonfiction Dead Move. The nonfiction book sets forth my theory in earnest, with no embellishments.

The primary purpose of Lethal Journey is to entertain. Accordingly, I have blended the best elements of my analysis with the murky legends of tradition. As I discovered in writing Dead Move, the true story is far more gripping than the legend of Kate and Tom Morgan. With Lethal Journey, I am able to ratchet the suspense as high as it will go. The reader should be aware that I do not believe some elements of the legend, and I had to add a few embroideries—but Lethal Journey is largely faithful to Dead Move.

The biggest difference is that Tom Morgan plays no significant role in Dead Move, whereas, in Lethal Journey, he is the murderous villain that legend has made him out to be. Wyatt and Josephine Earp really did live in the Stingaree, exactly as depicted. The dark lady at the Hotel Brewster is a fiction, though the Brewster really existed, and witnesses placed Lottie A. Bernard at that hotel. Other fictional elements include the Desmond Pinkerton, Secretary Babbitt, Peter Maurice, and Special Agents Dolbee and Collins.

On the other hand again, for example, Charlie Stevens of Star Stables really did take Lottie Bernard for a tour of the city, and Harry

West attended her exactly as shown here. She really did, for example, ask for an empty bottle and a sponge, and I am the first to suggest it was to make a pessary.

All these facts started tying together so obviously, once I had started assembling the many loose threads, tantalizing clues, and baffling dead ends of the true story as researched and related in the Heritage Department's official nonfiction book about the case. A.S. Gomer was the Chief Clerk, as mentioned.

John Spreckels really owned the Hotel del Coronado, and he was indeed with President Benjamin Harrison on a mission to save the Hawai'ian monarchy when Kate Morgan and her accomplices tried to blackmail him.

The blackmail is part of my theory, strongly supported in Dead Move. The story of the trunks (Kate's in Los Angeles, Lizzie's three in San Diego) is true. So are the families we know Katie Logan worked for in Los Angeles.

Katie Logan is truly documented as having told another maid at the Grants' house that her real name was Lizzie, and that she then corrected herself, stumbling, first saying she preferred Kittie, and then Katie.

Most importantly, in Dead Move I strongly explain that her death was a suicide. She really did write all those things on scraps of paper before she died—the invitations from famous actresses; the words I hardly know that man, I have only heard of him, which must refer to John Spreckels; and the enigmatic Frank Frank Frank Frank.

Regarding the latter, I took the liberty, with fun and delight, of having her meet L. Frank Baum. Why not? Baum did not, as far as I know, appear at the Hotel Del until after the publication and great success of The Wonderful Wizard of Oz in 1900. However, it is entirely possible that he visited San Diego in the decade previous, though it is unlikely he really met Lizzie. But you never know.

The words the golden atoms of the day were penned in the early 1600s by the Cavalier poet Thomas Carew as part of his poem A Song—here, the stanza:

Street names, some mentioned in the book, have not changed much in modern downtown San Diego. From the southern end of Balboa Park, on the park's western side, just north of A Street, the east-west streets run alphabetically as trees from Ash through Walnut. They are crossed by the numbered streets rising from downtown into Bankers' Hill.

The downtown streets begin at a line running east-west near the southern end of Balboa Park. They run east-west as the letters A through L. A Street runs parallel to, and just south of, Ash Street. At the south end of downtown, L Street is today a small piece running about four blocks, from near the Convention Center to Petco Park.

The numbered streets run north-south, starting east of Harbor Drive, Pacific Highway, and Kettner Boulevard. In Lizzie's day, the numbers were all designated as streets. Today, 1st through 12th are avenues, and the higher numbers are still streets. Where 18th Street should be is now Interstate 5, running north-south.

In Lizzie's day, today's Broadway was D Street, and today's Market Street was H Street. When Lizzie arrived in San Diego, she got off the train at the old California Southern Railroad Station on Kettner (pictured, at C Street). She walked east on C to the Hotel Brewster at 4th and C. The modern Union Station (opened as the Santa Fe Depot in 1915) stands on the same spot where, during the boom years, in 1887, the old station was built at which Lizzie arrived.

❧ ❧

Of the many fascinating twists to this story, one of the most remarkable is the so-called Mystery of the Missing Day.

Katie Logan, the house maid —reported missing in Los Angeles, and usually thought to be Kate Morgan under and alias, although there is powerful reason to think she was really Lizzie (she told another maid her name was really Lizzie)—bade the L. A. Grant family goodbye in the afternoon of Wednesday, November 23, 1892. The (also fake) Lottie A. Bernard shows up almost exactly 24 hours later at the Hotel del Coronado. Then, as now, the trip would take about two hours by train.

So where was she that whole time? Witnesses did report seeing her at the Hotel Brewster shortly before she arrived at the Hotel Del. Still, why care what she did during the missing day? Well, a witness named Joseph A. or Joseph E. Jones, who signed in right after her at the Hotel Del, told reporters he had seen her that morning on a train coming from Denver. He had noticed a man and woman having a commotion, resulting in many tearful apologies and entreaties from her, and his bolting off the train in a fit of anger. Jones, who was not subpoenaed to appear at the Coroner's Inquest, and who stated he wanted to avoid publicity, had no reason to lie. So how could she be on a train headed south from L.A. to San Diego, and simultaneously appear on a train headed west from Denver to Orange? Why go to so much trouble to make the huge detour suggested in my books? It can only have been out of her desperation and love for John Longfield— who saw Kate Morgan's blackmail scheme as a way to get rid of both Lizzie and the problem of her unwanted pregnancy. Longfield no doubt was motivated to go his extra mile (rather than cut and run back to Cleveland and Detroit) because Kate Morgan controlled him with what must have been her irresistible and wild sexuality. All these people disappear into history, but we can assume that Kate soon enough went her way after Lizzie's death, and John had no choice but to return to his wife and children in Detroit, after planting, for Kate, the implausible cover that Lizzie was alive and well in Toronto, and never planned to see her sister and mother again.

Another matter deserves closer scrutiny: the incomprehensible behavior of thousands of San Diegans— and, in fact, millions of Americans who breathlessly followed every rumor, every tidbit of truth, every scandalous insinuation of this saga from day to day in the nation's great newspapers, from New York to Los Angeles, from Chicago to New Orleans. Rumor and spectacle are understandably titillating, but why the vast circus of morbid sentimentality? Once we understand the Victorian mind a bit better, it all makes more sense.

Our mysterious, deceased 1892 beauty was on display for weeks in a San Diego mortuary while police orchestrated a nationwide search for her husband (who did not exist) and her brother (who was a lie) until, finally, they realized that the gorgeous and stylish Lottie A. Bernard herself was a total fiction. She had been found dead at the rear of the Hotel del Coronado after a 'sea storm of the century,' with a gun at her side and a bullet in her head, and nobody had any idea of who she was, why she had chosen this particular hotel, and why she had died there. All across the United States, newspapers great and small daily published the latest breathless telegraphic dispatches from San Diego. The stories were part fact, part rumor, and part dramas clattering in the purple prose of journalistic imaginations from typewriters inked with Yellow Press propaganda.

People who claimed to have known her contacted police—from Los Angeles, from Pasadena, from Detroit, from San Francisco, from Omaha, from all over the country. Various identifications were tried, of which the most promising was that of young Lizzie Wyllie, a beautiful young runaway from Detroit, pregnant by her married lover, a Ruined Woman in the most delicious Victorian tradition, and just as much a Fallen Angel—a pure and sublime female ideal, the embodiment of goodness, brought low by a coarse world and gross men (and women of low character).

Dark rumors swirled around her—that her husband, Tom Morgan, was a gambler who used her charms on Transcontinental Railroad cars to lure unsuspecting men into robbery and possibly even murder. She lay in state like the fictional dead princess in Maurice Ravel's famous 1902 piano composition Pavane pour une Infante défunte. Moderns wonder at this morbid spectacle, until one understands its roots. Among the Victorians, this grave sentimentality was a feature of their character—I think, a way of coping with the tensions of a universe of contradictions, in which one said one thing but did another, a world precariously balancing on a tightrope between an agrarian past and an urban future. London, the world's largest city at the time—possibly the largest city in the world since ancient Rome—was the clockwork and symbol of a newly industrialized civilization. At its apex, in turn, was a Queen and Empress, Victoria, after whose long (nearly 64 year) reign a world era would be named. She ruled from 1837 to 1901. In the 24th year of her reign, 1861, her young husband, Prince Albert, 42, died of typhoid fever, due to poor sanitation (and ignorance) in the royal residences. Deaths from preventable diseases were common among royals across Europe, which gives an indication of the mortality suffered by ordinary people and especially their children. The remaining forty years of Victoria's life and reign could be characterized as a cult of grief, in which she only wore black, and isolated herself in her royal estates. Prince Albert was enshrined at Windsor Castle until he and Victoria, after her death in 1901, were entombed in the royal mausoleum at Frogmore nearby. She dedicated monuments to him in London, like Royal Albert Hall and the Albert Memorial. Her life, thus, both flowed with, and to some extent set the tone for, the morbid sentimentality of the age. The mixture of emotional currents associated with Victoria (dark sentimentality, prudery, etc.) spread around the English-speaking world, including far-away places like San Diego. The classic White Anglo-Saxon Protestant Anglophile in the U.S. often referred to England as 'the mother country' (forgetting the long animosity of New England WASP farmer against this motherland, leading up to the American Revolution). Wealthy U.S. industrialists married their daughters off to penniless but titled English aristocrats (e.g., Consuelo Vanderbilt as Duchess of Marlborough).

During the 19th Century, displaced agrarian people thronged great new urban centers that were serviced by gas and electric lighting, central heating, paved roads, mass transportation, and complex water and sewage systems. As science and technology blossomed (the first modern gas-lamp in London is said to have been lit in 1816), sanitation, food preservation, and medicine struggled to catch up. The streets were still littered with horse droppings. In 1900, the average American lived about 49 years. Child mortality was crushing in its ubiquity and its tragedy. Death saturated every household. It was as yet a universe barely illuminated by modern understandings of theology and science. Death and judgment were, for most people, in the next room rather than somewhere in a distant future. For all the average person understood, the universe had been created only a few thousand years earlier. The farm itself represented a bloody, smelly, muddy universe of constantly evident birth and death in the keeping of animals and growing of crops (the Neolithic miracle of divine rebirth in grain)—all of this today sanitized from modern city life but, back then, a short walk or a quick ride away, and ever in the memories of people whose parents or grandparents might never even have seen a large city. And the city was, of course, wrapped in a pall of industrial smoke that made it seem like a Gothic purgatory.

ॐ ॐ

The dead girl in San Diego was the embodiment of a Victorian fetish. I say girl rather than woman, because she would be utterly pure in and of herself, and only defiled by gross people and circumstances beyond the self-control of her innocence.

The Fallen Angel was a Victorian trope represented in the work of many great artists, writers, musicians, and their schools. The Pre-Raphaelites were famous for their sentimental representations of historical myth, like Alfred Lord Tennyson's The Lady of Shallott (1833). The movement was a rebellion against the lurid, formal neo-Classicism of the French school of the late Bourbon monarchy.

The Pre-Raphaelites sought to replace faux Romanism in the arts with an earthier, more Nordic-Keltic-Arthurian ambience— hence, ladies drowning sorrowfully in inches of water, surrounded by lilies, or dying in castle beds surrounded by weeping Druids and so forth. John William Waterhouse, William Holman Hunt, and Dante Gabriel Rossetti were among the artists pouring forth these dark canvases whose tragedies were echoed in the streets and halls of 1892 San Diego. Charles Dickens (who also wrote of boy heroes like Tiny Tim in *A Christmas Carol*, and *David Copperfield* and *Oliver Twist*) created little heroines like

Amy in *Little Dorrit* and Sissy Jupe in *Hard Times*. Little Nell Trent in his 1840s' *The Old Curiosity Shop* weakens and dies, and crowds on Boston docks cause such a riot (yelling "is she dead?") that the captain of the ship bringing the latest installment of the journal hails them from off-shore, via megaphone, to tell them "She has died!" rather than risk having his ship swamped by a stampeding mob. In the United States, Stephen Crane (who would die in 1900 at age 28 of tuberculosis, one of the age's various horrid killers) created *Maggie, A Girl of the Streets* in 1893. The list of such artists and their creations is long. (It may even echo in many hard-boiled 20th Century novels, where the female lead is often objectified simply as 'the girl').

It was the age of Poe, who died young and tragically, and spent his life in drugs and drink, mourning the passing of his wife and cousin, and concocting dread tales (*The Pit and the Pendulum*) and poetry (*Ulalume*). It was the age of Byron, who eloped with his half-sister Augusta, and of Shelley, who drowned at Leghorn and was burned in Viking manner on the shore. It was the age of Mary Shelley, who lost all but one of her children in childhood, and died after a sad and stressful life at age 53—but not before, on a dark and stormy night in 1816 (the Year Without a Summer, owing to the explosion of Mount Tambora in Indonesia) she invented Frankenstein at a nocturnal party thrown by Lord Byron. That same night in the Villa Diodati, Lord Byron's physician, Dr. John Polidori (who died a few years later, 1821, probably a suicide) invented the modern vampire (Lord Ruthven). Later in the century (1897), Bram Stoker published his definitive Dracula.

Another real-life tragic heroine deserves mention, in connection with the Spreckels family and the events in Hawai'i concurrent with the story at the Hotel del Coronado that is told in the novel you have just read. In fact, we begin with another tragic hero of the age, the Scottish author Robert Louis Stevenson (1850-1894) of famous works like *Treasure Island*, *The Strange Case of Dr. Jekyll and Mr. Hyde*, *Kidnapped*, and others. Frail and beset with serious ailments, he sought a better climate in the South Pacific, and would ultimately die at 44 in the Samoan Islands. In the 1880s, he landed in Honolulu and befriended the beautiful and legendary Crown Princess Victoria Ka'iulani (1875-1899). She was the daughter of a Royal Hawai'ian mother and a Scottish financier, and designated heir to the childless King David. Traditionally, the Hawai'ian people had been ruled not by a central monarch, but by a powerful network of Royal Chiefs. All property was held in the name of these Royal Chiefs, and they elected their successors. Then, against their objections, amid mayhem and civil war in the 1780s, a powerful leader named Kamehameha the Great unified Hawai'i with himself as King. He and his successors adopted many European traditions, and managed to save their nation's sovereignty because it began to look a lot like a true nation in the Eurocentric sense. King David (1836-1891), for a time managed to resist the powerful U.S. missionaries who, together with U.S. corporate interests, tried to banish local customs, make people wear restrictive dark clothing, and—egad!—stop all that happy singing. King David, known as the Merrie Monarch, restored the hula dance and gave people back many of their rights and customs. He was the world's first monarch to travel around the globe, and was recognized by most of the world's monarchies including that of Queen Victoria in London. During the late 1800s, a German immigrant named Claus Spreckels made several fortunes in the U.S., culminating in the purchase of vast tracts of Hawai'ian cane sugar. He was a friend of King David, and became known as the Sugar Baron. The so-called Missionary Party, and their allies the Honolulu Bayonets and U.S. corporate interests—exemplified by Spreckels' rival, the so-called Pineapple King James Dole, cousin of missionary and future 'president' of a short-lived 'republic' of Hawai'i, Sanford Dole—conspired for years against King David's government. In 1887 they led a coup that installed the so-called Bayonet Constitution, depriving the king of much power. At the same time, they managed to dispossess the vast majority of Hawai'ians, on the theory that they had no right to their land because they did not have Western-style deeds of ownership. They also portrayed the native people as ignorant and brainless cannibals with bones in their noses (this, in the U.S. media and reactionary pulpits of the time), which helped allay any popular American objections to the eventual takeover.

King David became the first king to stay at the Hotel del Coronado. He dined in the Crown Room at Christmas 1890, a guest of John Spreckels, and then traveled north to San Francisco, presumably in Spreckels' yacht *Lurline*. He visited with his old friend Claus Spreckels (*père*) but died rather mysteriously at the Palace Hotel in January 1891. He was succeeded by his sister, Queen Lili'uokalani, who would be overthrown by U.S. and European corporate and missionary interests in January 1893. The succession would have gone to the Crown Princess, except the sovereign Kingdom of Hawai'i was no more.

The premature death of Crown Princess Victoria Ka'iulani's old friend Stevenson in 1894 was yet another blow, coming upon the death of the King in 1891, and the overthrow, treason trials, and other torments inflicted upon the doomed royal family at the hands of the European and American business owners, the Dole pineapple empire, and the Bible missionaries of which James Dole's cousin Sanford was the leader and the future ruler before annexation to the U.S. in 1898. Presidents Benjamin Harrison, a Democrat, and Grover Cleveland, a Republican, both tried to intervene on behalf of the monarchy, but without success (and very likely without sufficient energy or will). Crown Princess Victoria was at the time studying at a college near London, and returned hastily after the coup staged with U.S. Marines and Honolulu Rifles. Her work, petitioning the U.S. Presidents and Congress, and her efforts on behalf of many of her former subjects, now living in poverty and homeless, wore her down. When she traveled around the United States, her enemies in the Missionary Party widely portrayed her as a clown, a degenerate, a cannibal, and a heathen (her family had been Christian for generations). She was a cultured young woman who had been educated at the finest schools in Great Britain. She excelled in Latin, science, history, and sports. She spoke with the same refined accent spoken at Queen Victoria's court, and was far above the louts who constantly savaged her. Worn out, and hurt by other deaths in her family, she succumbed to stress and illness, and passed away in 1899 at age 24. She had been engaged to marry a young Hawai'ian prince.

She has been called the Peacock Princess because she loved her birds. It is said that when word spread of her death, the peacocks on her estate began screaming so loudly and incessantly in their grief, that servants finally had to go out and shoot all of the birds.

Such stories are background to our tale of Lottie A. Bernard, her true life of crime, and how she became a ghost. Some will continue to think of her as Kate Morgan, while others will be convinced by my theory that she was Lizzie Wyllie (pronounced like Wylie, of which it is a variant).

࿎ ࿐

Dressed in their finest, the city's womanhood came daily to spend hours with the dead woman's embalmed corpse at Johnson & Company Mortuary. She was the incarnation of that sentimental and tragic Victorian saint, the Fallen Angel. For a few weeks, the distant and shabby outpost of San Diego possessed that Holy Grail of all Victorian fantasies—a genuine tragic Fallen Angel.

Embodying the artistic and literary ideal of Tess of the d'Urbervilles, Little Nell, Maggie of the Streets, and a thousand other fictitious women, she had become flesh and died for the world to see. She was an unintended consequence of Kate Morgan's machinations, which have become enshrined in legend, although legend generally has Kate as victim and Tom as her murderer. I have taken a different tack in my 2008 analysis *Dead Move: Kate Morgan and the Haunting Mystery of Coronado, Second Edition (Nonfiction)*.

I based my carefully reasoned analysis on my own research and on the official research published [*Beautiful Stranger: The Ghost of Kate Morgan and the Hotel del Coronado* (HdC Heritage Department, 2002, 102 pp., ISBN 091625173X).] by the Heritage Department of the Hotel del Coronado, which they derived from copious reliable sources like the San Diego Public Library, the Coronado History Association, the San Diego Historical Society, the San Diego State University Library collections, and more. In my analysis, the presence or absence of Tom Morgan has no bearing on the plot Kate Morgan hatched, involving Lizzie Wyllie and Lizzie's married lover John Longfield.

In this novel, my goal has been to entertain you. I have combined the most exciting aspects of the traditional legend with the most logical revelations of my research. The result is a dark, crackling yarn that has me, as always, very excited by this great story. It is both a great San Diego tale, and a universal saga for men and women of all places and all times.

Police contacted Kate Morgan's grandfather asking how to dispose of the remains, and he wired back simply: "Bury her and send me the bill." He was obviously long disenchanted by her behavior.

When the ladies (and the gentlemen) of San Diego had finished adoring their Dead Princess, their Fallen Angel in her coffin, they organized a High Service funeral in the finest Episcopalian tradition. There was a great church service with flowers, a choir, priests in vestments with incense and liturgy, and all the city's gentry in gowns and black suits. There were tears, eulogies, and poetry readings.

When the ceremonies were over, she was forgotten that very day. After noon, her body was put in a plain wooden coffin on a wagon pulled by a donkey and driven (we assume) by a boy or an old man who got a coin for his services. Not a single mourner accompanied her on her final short journey to Mount Hope Cemetery on Market Street, outside the city limits at that time. She made her last trip alone, and was put in an unmarked (though numbered) grave without further ceremony or mention.

There the story would have ended except that, even today, people say the dead woman's ghost prowls the great hotel where she died. We might assume she is trying to tell us the truth about herself and what really happened—and that is probably very much like the story in this book.

From my nonfiction analysis in *Dead Move*:

The halls of the Hotel del Coronado are haunted as much by a loving mother's heart-rending cries, as by the ghost of a sweet and naïve young woman cut down in the flower of life. This very Victorian story leaves sentimental echoes in Coronado's balmy air, like a fading bloom of long-ago roses.

John T. Cullen
San Diego
January 11, 2009

About The Cover of <u>Lethal Journey</u>. The Hotel del Coronado's official Heritage Department book mentions, among many loose ends, a report that a handsome stranger visited the Wyllie home in Detroit a few times—no doubt John Longfield, whose relationship with Lizzie her sister May knew, but would have kept from their mother, Elizabeth. Longfield became a Detroit Police suspect after Lizzie's disappearance, and was found to have eloped with her. On one visit, he 'jocosely' made a statement May Wyllie later told to police, about picking roses in California—hence, the San Diegan rose on the front cover: "While you are freezing your feet in Detroit, I will be picking roses in California." The other rose in the image is not Lizzie Wyllie, but an unknown model for a Victorian postcard. Even in that guileless image, dangerous passion and unspecified tragedy seem to hover around her angelic features. Or is it just a weary sort of sadness? The picture, like the age that produced it, and the century that gave us Lizzie Wyllie, seems enigmatic when we look more closely.

Selected Reading:

Beautiful Stranger: The Ghost of Kate Morgan and the Hotel del Coronado by Heritage Department, Hotel del Coronado (Hotel del Coronado, 2002, 2005, etc.)

Dead Move: Kate Morgan and the Haunting Mystery of Coronado by John T. Cullen (Clocktower Books).

Coronado Mystery by John T. Cullen (Clocktower Books) contains the complete text of both Lethal Journey and Dead Move.

San Diego: California's Cornerstone by Engstrand, Iris (Ph.D.): (Sunbelt, 1980)

San Diego's Gaslamp Quarter by The San Diego Gaslamp Quarter Association & The San Diego Historical Society: (Arcadia, 2003)

The Story of New San Diego and of its Founder, Alonzo E. Horton by McPhail, Elizabeth C.: (San Diego Historical Society, 1979)

Online:

Website Coronado Mystery by John T. Cullen, including the Lottiepedia: http://www.coronadomystery.com/

Website of the San Diego History Center: http://www.sandiegohistory.org/

Website of the Coronado Historical Association: http://coronadohistory.org/

Website of the San Diego Police Historical Association http://www.sdpolicemuseum.com/

Notes

1. Note about Wikipedia: The 'Kate Morgan' entry at Wikipedia perpetuates the erroneous myth that the dead woman found at the Hotel del Coronado was Kate Morgan. I have independently concluded, without reference to any of this online material, that Tom Morgan appears not to have been involved in the crime. I have no comment on the Iowa background—interesting to some, but it has no direct bearing on the overall outcome of my research. The dead woman was not Kate Morgan, but Elizabeth 'Lizzie' Wyllie—as I have minutely and accurately detailed in this book.

2. The Legend of Kate Morgan: The Search for the Ghost of the Hotel del Coronado. By Alan M. May (ELK Publishing 1987, 1991) This book created a great deal of new misinformation, on top of the already baffling disinformation resulting from the 1892 cover-up of what really happened. Mr. May's book rekindled interest in the long-dormant story, which had been doctored into incomprehensibility by Spreckels' agents in 1892, and further suppressed by the hotel management over many decades. It should be noted that the Spreckels family owned the Hotel del Coronado until around 1948, after which time it was owned by various unrelated individuals or corporations. The Heritage Department appears to have published its excellent book Beautiful Stranger: The Ghost of Kate Morgan and the Hotel del Coronado in 2001 to counteract the misinformation of Alan May's sensational 1987 book. Mr. May's book caused local authorities to briefly reopen the investigation of 1892, but they quickly closed it, citing a lack of substantive new evidence in Mr. May's book. Mr. May died before actual publication in 1987. Mr. May claimed, among other things, to be descended from Kate Morgan (utterly unlikely), and that he, Alan May, regularly had dinner with the ghost in her former room at the Hotel del Coronado. The latter item, alone, should be enough to help the critical thinker and sensible reader draw their own conclusions.

3. The only two books I would recommend for reading about this true crime story are <u>Beautiful Stranger: The Ghost of Kate Morgan and the Hotel del Coronado</u> (official publication by the HdC Heritage Department) and <u>Dead Move: Kate Morgan and the Haunting Mystery of Coronado</u> (my analysis of the case, the nonfictional, scholarly companion volume to <u>Lethal Journey</u> which you are reading, first published in 2008). While the hotel's otherwise excellent book continues to support the misleading idea that Kate Morgan was the victim, my book strongly shows that the victim was Lizzie Wyllie. Kate Morgan was Lizzie's mentor, accomplice, and ultimately worst betrayer.